Boss Me Forever

Boss Me, Volume 1

Cameron Hart

Published by Cameron Hart, 2023.

BOSS ME FOREVER

First edition. September 12, 2023.

ISBN: 979-8227772602

Written by Cameron Hart.

Want a free book?

Sign up for my newsletter[1] and get your free copy of Chasing Stacy!

One look at the stunning waitress carrying the weight of the world on her shoulders, and I'm a goner. I wasn't looking for a sweet little thing with auburn hair and more baggage than I can fit on the back of my bike, but there's no going back now. She's mine. I'll prove to her I'm more than capable of handling her past and making her feel safe again.

---

1. https://dl.bookfunnel.com/7wbqvhsx8r

Connect with me!

Check out my website, cameronhart.net[2], for sneak previews on my latest projects.

Follow me on social media:

Facebook Page - facebook.com/cameronhartauthor
Instagram - instagram.com/cameron.hart.author
TikTok - tiktok.com/@author.cameron.hart
Goodreads - goodreads.com/16081533.Cameron_Hart
Bookbub - bookbub.com/authors/cameron-hart

Chapter 1

Declan

"Patrick, why did I get an email from Jung Hashimoto saying he was looking forward to our call, but since we missed it, he's decided to go with another agency?" I snap at my worthless assistant.

"Umm..." He stutters.

"Out with it, what did you do this time?"

"It's not my fault that you overslept. The call was this morning!" He protests. The whine in his already unpleasant voice is giving me a headache. I can already tell I'll have a migraine in an hour.

"The call," I grit out, "Was supposed to be for three-thirty."

"Right. I don't see what the problem is."

"Well, *Patrick*, the *problem* is that it's only ten in the morning. So why am I reading an email that was sent over five hours ago saying I missed an important business call?" I'm trying to rein my temper in. I swear I am.

"Yeah, well, if he was expecting you to call at three-thirty this morning, I could see why maybe Mr. Hashimoto went with someone else." He looks at me with a stupid little smirk hiding behind those beady brown eyes of his.

"Patrick," I seethe. "When I asked you to schedule the call for three-thirty today, I didn't think I had to specify it should be *in the afternoon*. Why the fuck would I schedule a call at three-thirty in the morning?"

"You said you were an early riser." He shrugs. "Plus, you know...Japan time?" He says as if it's a question.

That does it.

"Out!" I bellow.

Patrick's weaselly eyes go wide, but he doesn't move.

"I said, OUT! Get out of here, you're fired."

"But Mr. Knight, I—"

"I'll say it again since apparently, you have trouble understanding even the most basic of instructions. You are no longer employed at White Knight Advertising. As in, you will pack up your desk, collect your severance, and leave the building. I don't want to see you, I don't want to hear you, I don't even want to fucking *think* about you unless it's to tell my future assistants of your idiocy. Now, have I made myself clear?"

I should feel bad about making a grown man cry. But I don't. Guilt isn't something I have time to feel.

I watch Patrick stumble out of my office and grab up his few personal belongings. On shaky legs, he walks out of the office. Just in time for that migraine to hit me in full force.

I hear a slow clap start in the hallway, the sound making its way closer to me until it's in my office. I don't have to look up from my desk to know it's my younger brother, Cooper.

"Wow, how long did that one last? A whole two months? Is that a record or something?"

"Yeah, yeah, fuck you," I grumble.

"Did you have to make him cry though? That seems a bit harsh, even for you," he grins.

I don't dignify him with a response. Cooper, however, doesn't seem to need one.

"I mean, poor pot-bellied pat. How was he supposed to know three-thirty a.m. is an unreasonable time to have a conference call? The guy doesn't have much going for him anyway, and you go and take his job away too? Tsk-tsk, brother."

"Listen, could you give me a hard time later? I now have to find a new assistant on top of trying to win back the Hashimoto account."

Cooper winces at that. "Damn, *that* was the call you missed?"

"Yeah," I grunt.

"Well, then I guess that's probably why Asher is calling."

I look over at my cell phone perched precariously on the corner of my desk. Sure enough, Ash is calling.

"You can't avoid him forever. He flies in tomorrow night."

"Fuck," I say under my breath.

"Hey, look at it this way. If you talk to him over the phone, at least you'll be able to hang up on him." Cooper smirks at me. Most of the time he annoys me with his jokes and laid-back nature, but every once in a while, he pulls a smile out of me just when I need it.

"Asher," I say by way of greeting after putting the call on speaker.

"Declan, what's this about missing the call with Mr. Hashimoto?" He barks.

"Have you been hacking into my emails again?"

"It's not hacking if I got CC'd on the email," he grunts. "We really can't afford to lose out on such a big account. You know the board is looking very closely at the way we handle the business now that dad is gone."

I sigh. Like I need the reminder. The board has been breathing down our necks these last six months since our father passed away and handed the company down to his three sons. On the condition that the board approves, of course, and that we increase revenue by twenty percent in the first year. True to form, dad wanted the image of the perfect family dynasty but didn't actually have enough confidence in us to pull it off.

"Look, I'm going to fix it. I already started the process by firing my worthless assistant."

"Dammit, Declan. That doesn't look good, either. How many is that in this past year alone? Five? Six?"

"Seven," I grumble.

"We need to look stable right now, not rash and hot-headed."

"Hot-headed? The dumb fuck scheduled the call for three-thirty in the morning!"

"Well, did you specify you wanted it in the afternoon?"

Cooper snickers and I shoot him a glare.

"How the hell is this my fault? If the idiot—"

"Enough. It's a poor craftsman that blames his tools."

"Yeah, he was a tool alright," Cooper chimes in.

I smirk at him, thankful for his light-heartedness in the midst of the tense phone call.

"Cooper is there too?"

"Aw, shit," Cooper mumbles under his breath. My smirk turns into a full-on grin knowing I'm not the only one on the receiving end of our oldest brother's wrath.

"Listen, you two. I'm out here traveling the country, checking out our other offices, and trying to drum up more contacts for us, so I need you both to step up and keep things running smoothly at home base."

"Sir, yes, sir!" Cooper says in a mocking voice.

Asher sighs defeatedly, but I can almost hear him winding up for a fight.

I interject before this whole conversation goes off the rails. My migraine can't handle the inevitable shouting match my brothers would wind up in.

"Asher, I'm going to smooth things over with Mr. Hashimoto after I hire a new assistant. Cooper will continue the good work he's doing with research and development, and everything will be fine. You'll see."

"You have to stick with your next assistant, Declan. I mean it. The most important part of building a solid company is—"

"Building a solid team," both Cooper and I finish for him.

"We know, we know. We grew up with the same father you did, Ash," Cooper says with as much exasperation as a person could possibly muster.

"Well then act like it!" Asher snaps.

I'm about to tell Asher that we're all three co-CEOs, and therefore he has no right to talk to us that way when Cooper steps in.

"Ash, it's been a pleasure talking with you, as always. Declan and I feel so inspired by our little chat. Best to end on a good note. Have a safe flight, bye!" He hangs up on Asher before the guy can respond.

"That was fun," I say sarcastically.

"Aw, c'mon, it wasn't so bad. Plus, we got to hang up on him, which is always a treat."

I shake my head but can't hide my grin.

"You know, as much as it pains me to admit, Ash was right about something," he says.

"Oh?"

"You have to stop firing your assistants every time they breathe too loudly or walk in two minutes late."

"Jared didn't breathe loudly; he fell asleep at his desk and snored! And that woman, Susie? Scarlet? She was an *hour* late, and it was because her dog sneezed or something."

"Her dog ran away," Cooper corrects.

"Whatever. Late is late."

"You've gotta give people a chance, brother. Cut them a little slack."

"Yeah, like dad cut us slack?" I snap.

"Dad was an asshole, yes, but that doesn't mean we have to follow suit. He might have handed us his company with a ton of strings attached as a final fuck you to all of us, but we have a chance to make our own legacy here. Don't you want that?"

"When did you become so wise?" I mutter.

"I've always been the wisest one, Declan. I thought you knew that," he winks at me.

"That's not true."

"Oh, sure it is. Asher is the cold, calculated one. You're the hot-headed hardass. And I'm the self-aware wise one with the boyish good looks and charm for days."

I throw a pen at him, but he dashes out of my office and blocks it with the door.

"Love you, brother!" He yells from the hallway.

"Yeah, yeah," I mumble to myself.

I scrub my hands down my face and pull up an email to HR with a request for a new assistant. What a fucking day.

Chapter 2

"Lucas, are you up yet? I need to leave in thirty minutes if I'm going to drop you off at school and make it to my shift at the diner!"

I don't hear anything from my brother's room, so I knock again.

"Come on, I can't be late again. Frannie already hates me and I really need her to schedule me at least sixty hours next week!" After losing my second job as a telemarketer, I really need these hours.

Still nothing. I open the door in a huff but stop short when I see Lucas. He's pale and sweaty, and I swear he somehow looks thinner than I remember. He's always been skinny, but he looks like he's twelve, not seventeen.

Just then, he sits up and coughs. It's deep in his chest and rattles his body so much he has to suck in air.

"Lucas!" I rush over to him and grab the little wastebasket by his bed just in time to catch his vomit. When he's done, he looks up at me with tears in his eyes.

"Sorry," he coughs out.

"It's okay, no big deal," I tell him, hoping to calm him down.

Inside I'm freaking out. I'm worried about him getting sick again, about missing work, about his schooling. Even though I'm only three years older than him, I became his legal guardian last year when mom died suddenly of an aneurism. I dropped out of college and got the first job I could, waitressing at a diner by Lucas' high school.

A few months after mom died, Lucas was diagnosed with non-Hodgkin's lymphoma. It was a punch in the fucking gut, to say the least. Unsurprisingly, neither the waitressing job nor the telemarketing job came with any sort of health benefits, so I had to dip into the meager life-insurance money we got from mom's passing. And then I kept dipping into it. Again and again. Turns out having cancer is fucking expensive.

"I thought the radiation helped," I say softly, rubbing my brother's back. He had his last treatment a few months ago.

"I have good days and bad days," he shrugs. "I don't want to go back to the hospital."

"I know," I tell him. "But we have to get ahead of this thing, right? The doctors said if radiation doesn't work, we have to try out some other treatments."

"I'm sick of it! I hate watching everyone else play sports and go to prom and have normal fucking lives! I just want—"

His rant is cut short by another round of coughing. It breaks my heart, seeing him like this. His whole life has been upended, and try as I might, whatever I do never seems to be enough.

"Please don't fight me on this, Lucas," I beg.

He glares at me, but then his face softens. "What about work? You said you can't be late."

"Nice try, buddy. You're not delaying this. Your health is important. I can't lose you too."

Lucas looks stricken at my last statement. I should feel bad playing the guilt card, but I don't. If it gets him to the hospital, I'll play that card all day long.

He sighs and pulls the covers back, standing on shaky legs.

I clean out the wastebasket and call into work. Frannie is even less understanding than I thought she would be. In fact, she fires me. Which is just perfect. On top of figuring out medical bills and worrying about my sick brother, I have to find a new job. ASAP.

***

Six hours later, we're back home. Lucas is resting, while I'm frantically looking through job sites. I can't go back to service industry jobs with no health insurance. Not after the news we got today. Originally, they thought the tumors were slow growing, which is why they suggested radiation as a minimally invasive course of action. After a CT scan and an x-ray confirmed new growth in his tumors, one, in particular, that is close to his lungs, we all decided to move ahead with chemotherapy.

I expected Lucas to put up a fight, but he just sat silently in the chair next to me, the absolute picture of defeat. He didn't say anything on the way back to the apartment. He didn't even look at me.

At least he's resting now. The first chemo appointment is next week. He'll have one every day for five days and then rest for three weeks. Along with applying for jobs, I've also filled out a few applications for financial assistance with the new round of treatments. I cross my fingers and hope for some sort of break. I could really use a win right now.

I spend the better part of the afternoon skimming over job descriptions and salaries. There's not much in the way of well-paying jobs with regular hours and benefits for someone with only two years of college. Surprise, surprise.

One listing in particular catches my eye. For one, it has a crazy high salary, at least for me, and benefits. The best part is, they are looking to fill the position as soon as possible, which hopefully means they are willing to give someone like me a chance.

Plus, the office isn't too incredibly far away, so I can drive. Yeah, my brother and I are native New Yorkers, but our mom was a southerner through and through. She didn't like depending on taxis to get her where she needed to be. Mom would rather wait in traffic and pay for parking than jump in a car with a stranger, so she said. She made sure Lucas and I knew how to drive too.

I click into the job posting and see that it requires a four-year degree. My hope deflates a little, but I continue reading through the description. It's for an executive assistant at some advertising agency. The duties listed don't seem particularly difficult. Certainly, they don't require a college education, which is infuriating.

I have *excellent communication skills*. I can *manage time* with the best of them. Try working two jobs while taking care of a teenager who has cancer! I'll manage the shit right out of this executive's time!

Proficient in Microsoft Office products? This is 2019, who the hell doesn't know how to use Word and Excel? As for *organizational and prioritization skills*, let's just say my extensive book collection is in alphabetical order by last name of author, and my closet is arranged by color. And that's saying something. I love colorful clothing. And patterns. And accessories. Why be boring when you can be fabulous?

I take another look at the requirements and qualifications. There's no doubt in my mind that I can do this job, even though I'm not technically qualified. But fuck it, I need to step up and do *something* about my current situation.

So, I skim over my resumé and make a few...*tweaks.*

"Wrote down customer's orders and took them back to the kitchen." More like, *communicated the needs of the consumer to the business.*

"Worked twelve-hour shifts around taking my brother to all of his doctor appointments?" More like, *demonstrated the ability to manage time efficiently under pressure.*

With a few more "adjustments" to my resumé and one outright lie about graduating a year early with my business degree, I hit send.

Imagine my shock when my phone lights up an hour later with an email from the HR department of White Knight Advertising. I read it three times just to make sure. Yes, it definitely says they want to schedule an interview as soon as possible. It lists three times for me to choose from. I shoot an email right back taking the slot for tomorrow at four.

My tummy is full of butterflies. Yes, I'm anxious about my slightly less than honest application, but I'm also hopeful. For the first time in a really, really long time. Maybe this will be the start of a new chapter in our lives.

I rummage through my closet to find something remotely professional-looking, but I come up empty. I don't own dress slacks and all the skirts I have are either pink, teal, green, or covered in sequins. Yeah, I own clothes with sequins on them, so sue me.

I make a quick call to Sarah, my old college roommate.

"Luna!" She says excitedly. "Girl, what is *up*?"

Her greeting makes me smile. It's nice to have someone excited to hear from you.

"Sarah, have a big job interview tomorrow, and I was wondering—"

"If you could borrow something that the rainbow didn't throw up on?"

"Hey, now," I say, feigning offense. "I happen to like my colorful wardrobe. I seem to remember you borrowing quite a few things from me during freshman year!"

"Ah, yes, but I was young and foolish then," she teases.

"Just because you added black and white to your wardrobe doesn't make you old and wise, you know."

"No, but it sure helps me keep up appearances," she laughs.

I laugh with her, feeling lighter already.

"Well, can you help a sister out? I'm interviewing for an executive assistant position."

"How *fancy*," she notes.

"It has good benefits, which I need right now."

Sarah gets quiet, and I can tell I've brought the entire mood down.

"How's Lucas doing?"

"Not great," I tell her honestly. I give her the latest update. She listens and doesn't offer any pithy advice or empty encouragement. Instead, she says she has the perfect outfit for me to nail the job. We end the call after setting a time for me to stop by her place before the interview tomorrow.

I check in on Lucas, who is still sleeping soundly. I warm up some lasagna I made last night and eat it in bed while watching *Pretty Little Liars* on my laptop. Classy, I know. My eyelids get heavy before the episode is even over. The last thought in my head before drifting off to sleep is that tomorrow could change everything.

Chapter 3

Declan

"Thanks for your time, I'll be in touch."

Only, I won't, because this woman will definitely *not* be my new assistant. Nor will anyone else from the five interviews I've conducted today.

The first guy was promising, up until he said he'll need two weeks off next month to go to his sister's wedding. Who needs two whole weeks to get married? If it can't be done in a single evening, then the happy couple doesn't deserve to have guests, in my opinion.

The next lady was a complete mess, and the two after her were no better.

Then this woman sauntered into my office wearing a red dress that clung to her every curve. Her tits were practically spilling out and those heels she wore looked to be at least five inches tall. I've had former assistants hit on me before and I turned them all down. I'm looking for an executive assistant, not a hookup. Hard pass on Ms. Gold Digger.

I sigh in frustration and look over the resumé of the last interviewee of the day. She's young, but it says she has her degree. Her skill set and experience seem to line up with the job posting. Maybe a little too perfectly. Almost word-for-word. I have to chuckle at that. It's clever, really. I'm sure that's why HR set up an interview. They saw the keywords in her resumé and probably overlooked how young she is. Looks like Luna Foster gets some brownie points for her marketing skills. Honestly, if she's half as competent as her resumé suggests she is, I'll hire her. I haven't the time nor patience to start this whole hiring process over again.

Just then, there's a knock on my door. Our secretary, Tiffany, pops her head in.

"Declan," she purrs.

Ugh. Speaking of women who shamelessly throw themselves at me...

"Yes?" I say, maybe a little too harshly judging from the way she flinches.

"The next job candidate is here."

"Send them in." I take a deep breath and close my eyes, gathering up the last of my strength.

Please don't let this one be a dud.

When I open my eyes, I'm looking right into the face of a goddess. She has golden hair that falls over her shoulders in long, silky waves, pink, pouty lips, and huge, doe eyes. What color are they? It's not quite green, but it's not brown, either. Are those silver flecks in her irises?

"May I sit down?" The gorgeous creature in front of me asks. Her voice is smooth and solid. She carries a surprising amount of confidence for such a little thing. Tiny, really. But still curvy in all the right places. She's pocket-sized, and something about that makes me want to scoop her up and carry her with me everywhere.

Jesus, man. Get a hold of yourself.

I clear my throat and motion for her to take the seat in front of me.

"I'm Luna," she says after I still haven't been able to find my voice. I'm still reeling from my reaction to her. I'm turned on, yeah, but I find I want to protect her, know her, hear her every thought. Which confuses me almost as much as it pisses me off.

"Declan," I cough out. "Knight. Declan Knight."

She leans towards me and shakes my hand. Her skin is so soft, her little hand so delicate inside of my much larger one.

"Yes, I know who you are, Mr. Knight."

"Please. Call me Declan."

"Alright. Declan," she concedes, a small smile on her face.

Fuck, I like the sound of my name on her lips. On her tongue. I can think of a few other things I want in that pretty mouth of hers.

Dammit. Stop it right now.

"So, Luna. I see here you're just twenty years old."

"Well, I'd like to think I'm not *just* anything, but yes, I am twenty." She has a spark in those gorgeous eyes of hers, the hint of a challenge. Fuck if that doesn't make my cock twitch.

"And you recently graduated from college. This would be your first job?"

"This would be my first job in a professional setting, but I'm no stranger to hard work. I've waitressed and worked in marketing."

"*Tele*marketing," I correct. It's a dick move, but to her credit, she keeps her head held high.

"It's right in the name," she smirks. Usually, a smartass remark like that would piss me off, but coming from this little thing, it makes me want to smirk back at her. I don't, of course. I scowl instead.

I decide to stay on script since clearly this spitfire in front of me has the power to throw me off my game. I have some generic questions that HR emailed to me, so I read through those. Though, to be honest, I'm not really paying any attention to her answers. I've pretty much already decided to hire Luna. Usually, I like someone with experience, but I like the idea of training her just how I want her without having to break any bad habits.

Fuck, looking at her now, her confidence, sass, and curves all wrapped up in a tiny, tight little package has me thinking of other ways I want to train her. I'd tie her to my bed and make her beg for my fat cock. I'd drive her insane with teasing little kisses across her creamy skin. And then I'd bite her, mark her, before licking away the sting and sucking on every inch of that supple body until she's shaking with the need for release.

And then I'd make her hold it all in, driving her higher and higher until she can't stand it, until she's bucking and pulling on her restraints and crying for me to make her cum. Only then would I slam my dick into that tight cunt of hers and allow her orgasm to devastate her little body.

The only thing that pulls me out of those inappropriate thoughts is my dick swelling so much it punches my zipper, making me hold in a groan at the pain and pleasure.

Good thing Luna is still going on about whatever I just asked her. I've got to get myself under control. It's been a long time since I've had this reaction to a woman. Okay, I don't know that I've *ever* reacted to a woman quite like this before, but the point still stands. I haven't been with anyone since my father died, and even then, it was just a string of nameless women who knew what they were getting into.

"Luna," I say after adjusting myself and calming down a bit. "If I told you to schedule a call for three-thirty, what would your first course of action be?"

She looks at me with those olive eyes of hers and tilts her head to the side. "I suppose I'd see if your afternoon schedule was clear."

"You're hired."

Her eyebrows shoot up almost to her hairline, while her eyes are wide with shock.

"Really?!" She asks with such excitement it's almost contagious.

I nod in confirmation.

"Are you sure?"

"Are you trying to talk yourself out of a job?" I raise an eyebrow at her, fighting a smile.

"No, no, definitely not. Thank you, Mr. Knight. I mean, Mr. Declan. Um, Declan. Sir."

Jesus, hearing her call me *sir* has all of my dirty fantasies springing to life again. Not to mention other parts of me springing to life...

I stand before things get any worse down below and shake her little hand. Luna grasps my big paw and enthusiastically shakes it up and down, a brilliant smile making her already glowing face practically radiant. I find myself smiling back at her, which is a strange, new feeling for me.

"So, when can I start?" She asks, all bright and bubbly and too damn sweet. She looks so innocent in this moment, so fucking bright and young. I'm a dirty old man for having such filthy thoughts about her.

"Tomorrow?" I joke.

"Yes!" She all but shouts.

We're still shaking hands, a fact that Luna doesn't seem to register. I don't mind.

"Really?" I ask.

"Are you trying to talk yourself out of an assistant?" She winks at me, that spark from earlier lighting up her eyes.

"Tomorrow it is then," I say, still holding her hand.

As if suddenly realizing our less than professional handshake, Luna withdraws her hand from mine. For a tiny instant, I don't want to let her go. But I stuff that thought down and watch as she turns around and gathers her purse and jacket.

I lead her to the door with my hand on her lower back. I don't even realize I'm doing it until I hear her sharp intake of breath. I try not to think about what other sounds she can make with that mouth of hers. I swear, I'm trying to be good.

When we reach the door, Luna looks over her shoulder at me, her cheeks an adorable shade of pink.

Oh, sweet Luna. If you only knew the things I want to do to you.

I bet her face would be beet red. I bet it would reach all the way down to her perky little tits.

"See you tomorrow," she all but whispers.

With that, Luna walks down the hall towards the reception desk. I don't miss the way she fist pumps the air and wiggles her heart-shaped ass in a little victory dance.

I close my office door and lean against it, finally able to breathe again now that the siren is gone. With each intake of air, I get a little more clarity. I just hired a twenty-year-old. A beautiful, tempting, sassy, twenty-year-old.

And I can't fire her.

What the actual fuck was I thinking?

Chapter 4

Luna

By the time I get out to my old Nissan, I'm practically shaking with excitement. From getting the job, of course. And not because my new boss is sexy as hell and has piercing gray eyes that make my stomach do weird flippy things. Definitely not that.

So what if my knees went a little weak when I first walked in his office? I had to ask him if I could sit just so I didn't topple over. But it was probably just nerves. And not his strong, angled jaw, or his straight nose, or his full lips that curved in a small little smile when he looked at me for the first time.

I only blushed when he touched my lower back because, well, let's be honest, no guy has ever touched me like that. There was something so intimate about the way his large hand covered my back and slightly grazed over the top of my ass.

It made me wonder what his hands would feel like everywhere. Not that would know what any of that feels like. I've kissed guys before, but things never went any further than that. It's not like I'm saving my virginity for marriage or anything like that, I just want it to mean something. I'm not expecting forever, but I want to be with someone who matters. I want to matter to them, too. And so far, no one has ever kept my interest long enough to matter all that much.

This last year I haven't had the time or energy to think about dating or boys at all. But Declan isn't a boy. He's all man.

Stop it right now!

I manage to find a parking spot close to our apartment and hop out, ridding myself of all ridiculous thoughts about Declan and his broad chest, jet black hair, peppermint and pine scent...

Down, girl. He's your boss.

"Luna!" Lucas calls for me as soon as I close the front door. "How did the interview go?"

I walk over to his room and peer inside. He's got his little setup – tray of food on the bed, glass of water and a glass of juice on his nightstand, a stack of textbooks in the corner of his bed, long forgotten in favor of the videogame he's currently playing.

If he were a normal seventeen-year-old, I might scold him for being lazy. As it is, seeing him sitting up and engaging with the world around him means it's a good day.

Lucas pauses the game and looks at me expectantly.

I drop my shoulders and frown. His shoulders drop too, and he looks so sad. I sigh and sit down on the foot of his bed.

"I got the job," I say in the saddest tone I can muster. "And the worst part is, it pays really well and has great benefits."

"You got it?!"

I nod, solemnly.

He throws a pillow at me and I laugh, smiling brightly at him as I catch the pillow and throw it back.

"You're so mean!" He exclaims. "I'm sick, you can't tease me like that!"

"Don't play the cancer kid card on me. It doesn't work anymore. I'm immune," I say as I roll my eyes at him.

"Seriously, Luna, that's great. You won't have to work so many hours, right?"

"That's right. Just forty hours, maybe some overtime here and there."

He nods, and we're quiet for a moment. Finally, Lucas looks at me with such sincerity in his eyes. "I know I don't say it enough but thank you. You've given up so much for me."

"You'll just have to make it up to me when you get better," I tease, hoping to lighten the mood. His words mean everything to me, but if I dwell on them too much I just might cry. And that's not what I want to do. Not today. Not when things are finally looking up for us.

"Yeah, yeah, put it on my tab," he deadpans, though he can't hide his grin.

"What sounds good for dinner? I have to stop by Goodwill and pick up some professional clothes. I can grab something on the way back."

"You mean the office doesn't want you wearing glitter and sequins?" He asks sarcastically.

"It's something I hope to change soon, but for now I think I should play it safe," I wink.

He rolls his eyes at me in the way only a little brother can.

"How about Cowboy Rick's for dinner?"

"Perfect," I smile, thinking of our favorite Chinese place. It's a hole-in-the-wall restaurant that is all western themed, despite the traditional Chinese food it serves. We love it. So much so that I wonder if we're keeping the little gem in business.

***

The next morning, I wake up extra early to make sure I have plenty of time to get ready for my first day on the new job. I look over my outfit of choice in the mirror and debate which shoes to pair with it.

"*That's* your professional clothing?" Lucas says from my doorway.

"Yeah, so?" I say defensively. I take another look over the light teal pencil skirt and white blouse with big black polka dots on it.

"I mean, you look good..." He says, backtracking.

I laugh. "I tried to buy adult clothes. I swear I did. I even tried on a beige skirt. *Beige!* I mean, why is that an option? And why would someone choose *beige* over teal?"

Lucas just grins at me and shakes his head. "At least it doesn't have glitter on it."

"Exactly. Baby steps." I nod at him. "Are you going to be okay here?" I ask, changing topics.

"For the last time, I'm *fiiiiine*. Seriously, I'll just be playing video games all day." I open my mouth to reprimand him, but he throws his hands out in front of him in surrender. "Kidding, kidding. I know you talked to the school so I can do my classes online."

I give him a warning look as I walk out of my room and collect my things for the day.

"Okay, then. There are leftovers in the fridge, and I'm just a phone call away. If you—"

"Luna, chill. I'll be fine for a few hours. Now go on, get out of here so I can play video games," he winks, shoving me towards the door.

"Lucas!"

He snickers and then closes the door behind me. I wait until I hear the lock click, and then I head to the car.

It only takes me thirty minutes to drive to the office, which is pretty much a miracle in New York. Better still, my new job pays for a parking pass. I spend the first two hours of my day filling out paperwork, and then Tiffany, the front desk secretary, shows me to my new desk. It's right outside of Declan's office, which makes sense, but still makes me giddy. Much more than it should.

I steal a glance through the glass wall beside his door. Sure enough, the formidable man himself is sitting at his messy desk, phone in one hand, while pecking at his keyboard with the other hand. Just then, his eyes snap up to meet mine, almost like he felt me staring at him.

He skims his gaze down my body, but then looks angry and darts his eyes away. Does he regret hiring me already?

"Alright, so this is your space. You can log in with the credentials there on the sticky note," Tiffany says, pulling me back into the present.

"Great, thanks."

"Mmhm," she says. She sounds distracted, so I look up at her. Tiffany has her eyes trained on Declan, biting her bottom lip and leaning forward as if pulled towards him by a magnet. It shouldn't make me jealous, but it does.

"So, can I bring in photos and stuff? You know, personalize the space?" I ask, hoping to break her out of that lustful look she's giving Declan.

"Oh, I wouldn't worry about all that if I were you."

"Why?"

"Declan has a bit of a reputation around here. He doesn't keep assistants around for very long. He usually finds them..." Tiffany eyes me up and down. "... Lacking."

My jaw drops open at her rudeness, but I quickly recover. I vow right then and there to bring in a ton of shit to put up in my space, just to spite her.

"Noted. But I haven't disappointed anyone yet." I let the innuendo hang in the air. Hopefully, I came across as confident, though I'm feeling anything but.

Tiffany just scoffs at me and walks away, her heels clicking on the floor.

I get caught up in learning Declan's schedule and figuring out how his last assistant organized things. If this clusterfuck of a calendar is any indication of the quality of work the last person did, no wonder they got fired. I'm already bursting with ideas on how to more efficiently organize things and communicate more effectively. I'll prove Tiffany wrong. I'll outlast all of Declan's previous assistants.

"Luna," a deep, silky voice startles me from my work. I know who it belongs to even before I look up, so I'm not surprised to see Declan standing in front of me.

I am, however, surprised at the look he's giving me. It's cold and distant. So different than the man who interviewed me yesterday, the man whose touch made my heart literally throb...as well as other, lower parts of me.

"Declan. Sir," I address him. His eyes flash with something, but then quickly go back to the hard as steel look he was giving me before.

"I trust you are learning the ropes around here and that I don't need to hold your hand through every single thing."

I'm still taken aback by his icy tone, but I don't let him fluster me. If this hot and cold game of his is what made his other assistants snap, then I'm all the more determined to remain professional and rise to the challenge.

"I believe I see why your last assistant didn't live up to your expectations," I tell him in as smooth a voice as I can muster. Declan looks amused for a second but then schools his features. "I already have a few ideas on how to restructure—"

"I don't need to know the details, just make my life easier and let your work speak for itself."

With that, he raps his knuckles on my desk and goes back into his office, slamming the door shut.

Oh, I'll let my work speak for itself, alright. I'll be the best damn executive assistant he's ever seen.

Chapter 5

Declan

I had a shit night of sleep thinking about little Luna in her polka dot blouse and teal skirt. Why that ridiculous outfit turned me on so much is beyond me. It took until two in the afternoon to make my dick stand down after just barely looking her up and down through the glass wall in my office. I waited another hour before venturing out of my office and checking in on her.

I'm pissed at myself for hiring her, and even angrier that I can't seem to control my body's reaction to her. Then she went and called me *sir* and all but called my last assistant an idiot. Both of those things drew me closer to her. And then she got all excited about her ideas for efficiency. That little spark in her eyes telling me she couldn't wait to prove herself had my cock lengthening in my slacks again, and I had to walk away.

God, those olive eyes of hers were so full of innocence. She's fifteen years younger than me. She's a bright, bubbly force to be reckoned with. And I don't need that kind of complication in my life.

I sigh and lean against the back of the elevator on the way up to the office. I rub my temples, hoping to ward off the fogginess in my head before the day has even started. The elevator door dings and opens up to my floor.

I don't even take ten steps into the lobby before my eyes are assaulted with pink. So much pink. I had no idea there were so many shades of pink, but apparently, there are. And Orange. And yellow. The explosion of color hurts my eyes and gives me an instant tension headache. All of it is coming from one little miss Luna's desk.

She brought in an orange fleece blanket, a pink throw rug, and pink picture frames. There's an honest to god yellow fuzzy bean-bag chair in the corner of her cubical. She has a bright pink dry erase board, a pink bulletin board, a pink stapler, pink sparkly mousepad, an assortment of pens with feathers sticking out of the end organized by color. She even has a fucking sequined pillow on her office chair.

Just then, Luna pops up from under her desk, where I see she has plugging in a lava lamp. With, you guessed it, pink lava.

She smiles brightly at me and waves enthusiastically. Is having too much color a good enough reason to fire someone? I'm guessing not. Shame.

"Morning, Declan!" She says all too cheerfully. And I thought the sequined pillow was loud.

I grunt at her and walk into my office. It's too damn early for this much color. And sound.

It's only for a little while, I remind myself. Just until we go over the end of the year financials with the board.

I open up my email, expecting the usual barrage of a hundred different requests, either from clients, potential clients, or employees. Only, I don't see any of that. Instead, I open my inbox and see four separate folders.

"What the hell?"

Just then, there's a knock on my door. I already know who it is. She doesn't wait for me to answer, Luna just waltzes right in, coffee cup in hand.

"Hi. I noticed you aren't a morning person, I thought coffee might help. You've got a busy day today! I mean, I suppose all of your days are busy. But today, hopefully, I can help."

I eye her up and down, taking in her royal blue dress pants and yellow, frilly blouse with orange and blue swirls up the sleeves. Where the hell does this girl shop? And why are her preposterous outfits such a damn turn-on?

"My email is all fucked up."

"Oh, good, so you've already seen some of the changes I'm implementing!" She either doesn't catch the fact that I'm less than thrilled with this new development, or she ignores it completely.

"You'll see here, instead of the chaotic casserole of emails all jumbled in one place, I created these four folders that automatically organize each email as it comes in. The *Internal Emails* folder are those from employees, *New Client Inquisitions* is self-explanatory, then *Open Threads* is when an email has been responded to and requires a response back from you, and the last one is *Junk*, which, again, self-explanatory."

I'm not sure what to say to all of that. It makes sense, but I still feel like my privacy was violated. That being said, her new system does seem…efficient. I almost want to compliment her, but instead, I say the first thing that pops into my head.

"Chaotic casserole?"

"Yeah, you know, like when money is tight, but you still need dinner, so you throw whatever veggies and canned goods you have in a casserole dish, add rice and water, stick it in the oven and hope for the best?"

I stare at her for a second, not sure if I want to laugh or be annoyed with her ridiculous comparison of my inbox to her casseroles.

"Um, or maybe that was just my mom. You probably had someone who cooked all of your meals for you, huh?"

Annoyed it is. I don't dignify her with a verbal response, opting instead to glare at her.

"Anyway," she continues after her little outburst. "The email organization was the first thing I wanted to show you."

"There's more?" I grunt.

"Yes! So glad you asked." She grins at me. The little brat. I want to bend her over my desk and spank the sass right out of her.

Well, shit. That's an image I won't get out of my head for the rest of the day.

"I installed a project management app on your desktop. I have it on my phone as well, and I'd like for you to install it on your phone."

"Excuse me?" Is she really telling me what to do right now?

"It's really quite intuitive. Basically, you or I can put in projects and add other people as necessary. You can rank tasks as high, medium, or low priority, put in deadlines, reminders, all that stuff. It will help us communicate and have transparency. That way I know what things are most important to you day-to-day while at the same time I can keep an eye on the longer-term projects."

"You seem to have forgotten that I'm your boss. You answer to me," I tell her harshly.

She stares at me, brow furrowed, head cocked to the side. I ignore the way her confused expression tugs at something in my gut.

"I'm just trying to help..." She says, each word so sincere I almost feel bad about what I'm going to say next. Almost.

"That's right. Your job is to *help* me. You are to make my life easier, not more complicated. Did you even think to ask my permission to hack into my email? Or download things on my computer? If I wanted a new workflow, I would have asked for it."

"Would you?" She shoots back, that fire blazing in her eyes. I'm equal parts furious and turned on. I lean into the anger.

"What the hell does that mean?" I snap, almost yelling at her.

She flinches and actually looks like she might cry. Fuck, fuck, fuck, why does that expression on her face make my chest tighten?

But then her nostrils flare and her jaw tenses. She balls her tiny fists up and plants them on her hips. Yes, bring it on, little Luna. Give me your fight, your fury.

"Did you ever think maybe the reason your last *seven* assistants didn't work out is because of *you*? One or two duds, I would understand, and the guy before me seemed a bit dense, I'll give you that. But maybe you're frustrated and floundering because of your own shortcomings, and not because of whoever happens to be sitting at that desk outside of your office."

My dick is leaking in my boxer briefs as anger swirls with arousal in my veins. No one talks back to me like that, aside from Asher. I hate that I want to fuck this little spitfire into submission, but more than that, I hate how much sense she's making.

"It's the job of my assistant to anticipate my needs and to cover for my *shortcomings*," I grit out, fists clenched on top of my desk.

"And that's what I'm trying to do!" She yells in exasperation. "I'm trying to be proactive and put systems in place so I can see what gaps need to be filled in!"

We are at a stand-still, Luna and me. What happens next will determine our boss/assistant relationship. I have every intention of putting her in her place and cutting her down with my words.

Instead, I watch my hand grab my phone and unlock it. As if under a spell, I see my fingers moving over to the app store and navigating to the project management app she already has on my computer. I listen as she tells me the login information, and type it in.

What the actual fuck is happening? How did she get the upper hand so quickly?

She bends over my shoulder and shows me around the app, how she has my schedule and major projects already loaded in there, how I can click into each project, and create to-do lists and deadlines. She goes on and on, but I'm still in a trance. She smells like oranges because of course, she does. I turn my head and take in her profile while she continues to tell me about the wonders of the app.

Luna doesn't wear much makeup, and she doesn't need to. Her eyelashes are naturally long and full, her lips a pretty pink that make me wonder if her nipples match. She has a delicate little nose that scrunches up as she says something about not liking a particular feature in the app.

I watch with rapt attention as she tucks some of her silky blonde hair behind her ear. Then, Luna bites her bottom lip and turns her eyes on me. I realize she must have asked me a question or something.

"Sir?"

Jesus fucking Christ, she really has to stop saying that.

Instead of letting her know I was too distracted by every goddamn thing about her to pay attention to her little spiel, I nod and set my phone on my desk. She takes the hint and backs away, walking towards the door.

Except, I don't want her to leave just yet.

"Luna," I call out, my voice so deep and gravelly it surprises even me.

"Yes?"

"My coffee is cold. I need a fresh cup."

Her shoulders drop a little, letting me know I hit my target. Yeah, it's an asshole move to reduce her to an errand girl after she just reorganized my entire professional life in what I'm sure will be a profound way, but this is only her second day. I can't let her get too big for her britches, so to speak.

Luna walks over to my desk and grabs my cup without a word. I bite back a groan as she turns around and walks away. She's not trying to be sexy, but the sway of her hips and that tight ass of hers has me losing my fucking mind.

"Anything else?" She asks in the fakest sweet voice I've ever heard anyone muster up. It almost makes me grin. I like knowing I got under her skin. It's only fair. She's burrowed her way under my skin in less than forty-eight hours.

"That will be all," I say dismissively. She huffs out a little indignant breath and shuts my door a little too forcefully.

Once she's back at her desk, I spin my chair around so no one can see me and whip my aching cock out. I fist myself and stroke once, twice, three times, and then explode into my hand like a fucking sex-starved maniac.

What the fuck have I gotten myself into?

Chapter 6

Luna

Lucas has his first chemo appointment is today, and I hate that I'm missing it. After my rocky second day with Declan, I didn't think I could afford to ask for a morning off. I've been with White Knight Advertising for a week and a half now, and I've hardly spoken to Declan since. After going toe to toe about the emails and project management app, I've barely seen him aside from sitting in on meetings and taking notes. He doesn't look at me or even acknowledge me in those meetings, and I simply email him my notes when all is said and done.

From what I've gathered, he's not one much for compliments, but he's quick to tell you if you're fucking up. So far, aside from our one argument, he hasn't told me I'm fucking up. I'll consider that a job well done. A part of me is disappointed in the way things have turned out. I mean, I know it's for the best. Declan is a bit of a cold-hearted jerk, despite my best efforts to go above and beyond my job description and help him out before he even knows he needs help.

My phone rings, breaking me out of my thoughts. I take my phone call out in the hallway so as not to disturb the others.

"Lucas! How did everything go? How are you feeling? Do you need me to come home? Can I pick up some juice or something?"

"Luna, calm down," he reassures me. His voice sounds weak, but at least he's chuckling at me. I can almost see him shaking his head at all of my worries. "It was fine, they did it through an IV, so I don't have to have a port put in or anything. I'm just feeling a bit weak."

"I'm so sorry I wasn't there, Lucas."

"Psh, who says I would have let you come anyway?" He teases. "You're working so hard and I know it's all because of me. I really do appreciate this, Luna."

"There you go getting all sentimental on me again," I try to joke, but I don't quite pull it off, seeing as I have to wipe a rogue tear from my cheek.

"Yeah, yeah, maybe it's a side effect of the chemo?"

We both laugh at that. "I'm glad you're doing okay. I'll be home as soon as I can."

He agrees, and we say our goodbyes. I take a few minutes to collect myself. Everything about being a caregiver is exhausting, even on the good days.

When I get back to my desk, I see Frank poking around, clearly waiting for me to return. He's nice enough, from the research and development team.

"Hey, beautiful," he says, giving me a too-eager grin.

"Hi, Frank." I try not to be rude, but I just can't deal with him right now.

"Why so stressed? Declan being an asshole again?"

"You know his office is right there," I point behind Frank.

"That's not a no, gorgeous."

I roll my eyes at his names for me. They should be sweet, I guess, but they make my skin crawl coming from him. I'm more than just a pretty face, and even that is in question half the time.

"Is there something I can help you with?" I ask, hoping to change topics.

"As a matter of fact, I was hoping you'd go to lunch with me. It's about time we got to know each other outside of the office, don't you think?"

Frank scoots closer to where I'm sitting in my chair. He's still leaning on my desk, and now his leg is brushing up against mine.

"No, thanks, Frank. I've got a lot to do here today."

"You have to eat, Luna. So why not eat with me?"

"I'm not hungry right now, thanks though." I turn on my computer and get to work, doing my best to ignore him until he goes away.

And then his hand is on my knee. I recoil from his touch, but he grips my leg tighter.

"I'm trying to be nice here, beautiful. You wouldn't want to start off on the wrong foot with anyone here, right?"

"I think you should go, Frank. Please, let go of my leg. I don't want to go to lunch with you," I tell him firmly.

"Why the hell not?" Just then, Frank is pulled away from me.

"She said she doesn't want to go to lunch with you, now respect her wishes and get the fuck out of here, Frank."

This is the closest Declan and I have been in over a week. He's much taller than Frank, and he's currently gripping Frank's shoulder in a punishing hold while shoving him down the hall. When he turns towards me, I see his anger melt away and looks at me with...concern?

"Are you alright, Luna?"

I nod, taking a deep breath. "Yeah. Not the first time some creep hit on me," I try to laugh it off.

Declan's eyes harden and he clenches his jaw tight. "You shouldn't have to deal with that in the workplace. I'll make sure Frank is taken care of."

"It's really not that big of a—"

"Enough. He'll be dealt with. Now, let's go to lunch."

Despite everything that just happened, I fight a smile. The first time this big, intimidating, growly man has spoken to me directly in a week and he's shooing off a creeper and then demanding that I go to lunch with him. The same thing Frank wanted and got rejected for.

Something about Declan though exudes confidence and power. Not in a way that he would use it to his advantage, like Frank, but in a way that says he works hard for what he wants. And what he wants is to have lunch with me.

Declan stands in front of my desk and waits for me to gather my things, knowing that I would go with him. It should infuriate me, the way he ordered me to lunch, but I find I don't mind. In fact, I kind of like him telling me what to do.

He guides me towards the elevator with his hand on the small of my back, like the first day in his office. Also like that first day, his touch has my body doing all sorts of things like tingle and tighten and blush.

Get a hold of yourself, girl!

Chapter 7

Declan

Luna plays with the hem of her flowy teal skirt and fidgets nervously in the seat beside me. I don't know what came over me when I saw her with Frank. Seeing him talk to her had me growling, fucking *growling* at my desk. I felt like a rabid, delusional dog. But I was holding myself back because I realized I was being ridiculous. I have no claim on this woman, however much she's captivated me. It's not fair for me to feel possessive. But then he touched her and I fucking snapped.

I was over there in half a second, ripping the bastard off of her. I saw where he was gripping her leg and I wanted to punch his fucking face in for hurting her. Touching her. Looking at her.

Jesus, I wanted to break every bone in the hand he had on her thigh. But then I looked over and saw Luna fighting through her fear, trying to be strong, and I knew she didn't need this situation to escalate. He'll be fired at the end of the day, and that has to be good enough for now.

I'm not sure where the invitation to lunch came from. Well, I didn't so much *invite* her as I *told* her, but still. It pleased me very much that she instantly got up and followed me out. Frank was turned down for the very same request, yet here she is, in my car, on the way to lunch.

I told the driver to take us to Le Coucou, a French bistro that is normally difficult to get into without knowing the right people. Good thing I know the right people.

We hop out once my driver pulls up, and I resume my position beside Luna, one hand on the small of her back. I can't explain the urge I have to touch her and feel her warmth.

The maître d' pulls out a chair for Luna, but I give him a glare and he scampers off. I push her chair in for her. Luna doesn't seem to notice my sudden caveman behavior, which is just as well.

Sitting across from her now, I take in every single thing about her. She's busy studying her menu, while I'm busy studying her. Those rosy cheeks of hers are killing me, along with her tiny nose. She's like a fucking doll. Luna's big, expressive eyes roam over the menu, her lovely lashes fluttering ever so slightly when she comes across an unfamiliar dish. She worries her bottom lip with her teeth, which makes my dick twitch.

Luna sighs and puts her menu down. "What do you normally get?" She asks.

"I thought we could start with crème de concombre. Then maybe..."

Luna furrows her brow, which is too cute for me not to grin. She looks a little lost, and for the first time, I notice she's trying to hide her loud pink blouse under her more conservative black coat. She's clearly uncomfortable here, which is not what I want. It does something weird to my chest, thinking about Luna hiding away. As if she could, anyway, but I don't like that she wants to.

"Is there somewhere else you'd like to go?" I ask.

Instantly, her shoulders loosen, and that bright smile is back on her face. I didn't realize how tense she was before, but now all of that is gone.

"Oh, yes. I have a great place in mind. You're going to love it, everyone does."

The girl almost knocks her chair over in her hurried escape from the restaurant. I have to chuckle at that. How many women would kill to be in her position right now, at one of the most exclusive restaurants with one of the city's most eligible bachelors? Luna sure isn't like any woman I've ever met.

I leave two-hundred dollars on the table for the restaurant's trouble of finding a place for us on such short notice and follow Luna out. She skips her way to the car, teal skirt and pink shirt blowing around her in the breeze. She looks like a tiny hummingbird. *My* hummingbird.

Where the hell did that come from?

Luna slams her door shut, saving me from my train of thought. She guides my driver closer to our office and has him drop us off a few blocks away. He gives me a skeptical look in the rearview mirror, but I nod him off. I have no idea where she's taking me, but if worse comes to worst, we can just go back to the office and order in.

"It should be around here somewhere..." Luna says to herself.

"Do you not know where this restaurant is?"

"Of course. It just moves around," she says as if it's obvious. It is not obvious.

I follow her down the block and then we turn the corner.

"Ah hah!" She exclaims. I'm not sure what I'm looking at, but her joy is contagious. "There, Paco's Tacos!"

"I don't see the restaurant."

"It's a food truck!"

Before I can even process the fact that I could be having fried oysters right now instead of food from a *truck*, Luna takes off to stand in line. I follow her, not liking this feeling of her being in the lead. She's in control now. And I just handed it right over to her.

"Now, I know what you're thinking," she says once I'm beside her in line. "*A truck, Luna? Really?*" She says in her best imitation of my voice. "But let me just say, these are the best tacos in the city. And if tacos aren't your thing, then honestly, you don't deserve to eat."

I find myself grinning down at this little spitfire.

"I like tacos," I tell her.

"Phew! You're not a lost cause after all."

I should be offended at her comment, but I'm not. I've fired people for less. Literally.

Her sass, excitement, and even the damn bright outfit she's wearing has me feeling all sorts of things about her.

"I think it's our turn to order," I say, hoping to get these strange new emotions under control.

She smiles and orders for us, but once again I'm not listening to her words. I'm simply taking in her beauty and trying not to haul her into my arms and brush my lips against hers.

I manage to keep my hands to myself, but only because she insisted I grab one of the tables scattered around once it opened up. A few minutes later, Luna sets down several plates stuffed with tacos of every kind. There have to be at least twelve tacos here.

"Did you get one of everything?" I tease.

She shrugs. "You were buying," she smirks at me. "Plus, there were some tacos I haven't tried yet. Whenever I come, I don't want to risk getting a new taco on the chance it's a dud, so I stick to the three that I know are good."

Her response is refreshing and honest and makes me smile again. Luna doesn't hesitate to dig right in once she's seated. Her eyes shine as she looks over the available tacos, and then she puts three on her plate. I follow suit, but then pause when I hear her moaning. Fucking *moaning* as she devours her first taco.

Jesus, how can she make eating a damn taco look sexy?

"What? Do I have something on my face?" She asks, pulling me out of my trance.

I clear my throat. "No, nothing," I mumble. I never mumble. What is she reducing me to?

Luna shrugs and takes a sip of water. "So," she starts. "How did you get to be CEO of such a large advertising company? You look so young." Her face turns pink, which is fucking killing me. "I mean, not that like you're *too* young. I'm sure you're qualified and everything. Sir," she adds at the end.

She looks flustered, and I won't lie, I like that. I enjoy watching her squirm a little. At least I know I have some sort of effect on her, too.

"My brothers and I run the company. Asher, the oldest, is constantly running around and acquiring new clients, as well as checking up on our other branches. I handle contracts and negotiate terms, as you know, and the youngest, Cooper, is head of research and development, as well as special projects. The three of us have always worked for the company – it was our father who started it all."

"Oh, I didn't realize you were part of a family dynasty," she teases.

"Yeah, well, the old man died a few months ago and left it to us." It comes out more bitter than I mean it too, and I wish I could take it back. I watch Luna's face fall. I'm used to getting pity from people, but that's not what I see on her face. Good thing, too, because for some reason she's the last person I want to pity me.

"I'm so sorry," she all but whispers. "I lost my mom last year. It was totally unexpected, and...well, I'm just so sorry."

Shit, I didn't mean to bring up bad memories for her. Instinctively, I reach out for her hand. My father and I had a complicated relationship, but even so, it was hard losing him. From the looks of it, Luna had a much better relationship with her mom. I'm sure her pain is much deeper than mine.

Luna startles a little when my hand covers hers, but she doesn't pull away.

"You were close with your mom?"

Luna smiles, though it doesn't reach her eyes. "Yeah, she was my best friend. I know that sounds lame, to have your mom be your best friend at my age, but she really was."

"It doesn't sound lame. My mom was too busy being a socialite and cheating on my dad to care about my brothers or me. The best thing she ever did for us was move to the Cayman Islands with her barely legal boyfriend."

Fuck, why did I say all of that? What the hell is wrong with me? My dad and I didn't see eye to eye on much, but we both agreed that vulnerability is a weakness. Here I am just giving her all the power. I hate it. I withdraw my hand and ignore the cold feeling that washes over me at the loss of contact.

Luna looks absolutely stricken by my confession, which has more foreign emotions bubbling up inside. I must have sprung a leak deep down in my soul, but it's time to patch it up and put up another wall.

I clear my throat and ask her about lighter topics, like college and her hobbies. She likes reading and working on crafts like scrapbooking and crocheting, which somehow fits her perfectly.

"Wow, we did good work here, huh?" She asks, surveying the trays that once held tacos.

"We did indeed," I reply, that grin playing at my lips again, the one that I can't seem to stop when I'm around her. "You were right, those tacos were pretty damn good."

"*Pretty* good?!" She asks incredulously. "No offense, Declan, but I take my taco consumption very seriously, and I promise you, those are *the* best."

I hold my hands up in surrender.

"You know what's almost as good?" She asks playfully.

I shake my head no.

"The churros." Luna lifts one eyebrow up, almost daring me to try them. Sneaky girl. Of course, I'd buy her a churro. I'd buy her a hundred churros. They are only a dollar, after all.

"I'll be the judge of that," I tell her before making my way back up to the food truck. Luna follows taking care of our dirty dishes on the way.

A few minutes later, we have piping hot churros in our hands.

"Wanna take a walk? Let our food settle?" She asks. I know I should get back to work. I have an important client to win back.

I open my mouth to tell her as much, but instead, I find myself saying, "Lead the way."

Luna gives me a shy smile and turns her head away from me so I don't see the blush on her face. Little does she know, her blush reaches all the way to her ears and down her neck, so I see anyway.

We walk in silence for a bit, munching on our churros, which are indeed, delicious. I'm not one much for sweets, but I can see how these might be addicting. I have every intention of turning around once we've finished and thrown our wrappers in a nearby trashcan, but for some reason, my feet keep right on moving in step with hers.

Luna tells me more about her mom, though I can tell some of the memories are still painful for her. She talks about her brother and the pranks they used to play on each other growing up. She tells me about the time she found a cat and brought it inside and hid it in her room. She fed it her leftovers for days until it got out and her mom screamed and told her it was a raccoon.

The whole time I'm silent as I listen to her and watch her animated hand gestures, the way her expressive face lights up.

Finally, she turns to me. The sight catches me off guard. I knew she was sexy, and her curves called out to me, but in this moment, she is simply beautiful. Innocent. Vulnerable. She is pure goodness.

"Sorry I've just been going on and on. It's nice to have someone—"

She's cut off by a biker who whizzes by and clips her on the elbow. She stumbles into me as I reach out for her. Fuck, the way her soft little body presses into my chest has me practically growling with possessiveness.

Some primitive and primal part of me takes over. I grab her hips and walk her backward into the alley just a few feet away. Pressing her into the wall, I look down at the goddess still in my embrace. She looks up at me with those big doe eyes. I see her chest heave with shallow breaths as her pulse quickens on the side of her neck.

My hand skims up her left side, following the dip of her waist and the curve of her breast. I cup the side of her face and brush the pad of my thumb over her lips. She parts them so sweetly for me.

"What are you doing to me, little Luna?" I whisper, more to myself than to her.

"The same thing you're doing to me," she breathes out as her hands move from my biceps to my chest, where she fists my shirt.

Fuck, I know I shouldn't do this. She's my assistant, for Christ's sake. She's fifteen years my junior. She likes lava lamps and crocheting, and she's oddly opinionated about tacos. I can't. And yet...

I lean down, closer, closer, closer to my temptation. I'm inches away from her sweet lips when she turns her head to the side.

"We can't..." she murmurs. Her words say one thing, but her body says another. I can feel the heat of her pussy, and I know she feels my hard cock on her soft little stomach.

I'm frozen in place, my muscles tense with the need to claim her, to own her, to dominate her, to bring her to the brink of pleasure and the throw her right over until she's drowning in ecstasy.

I know she wants it too, but she's stronger than I am. Luna releases my shirt and slips away from me.

"We should probably get back to the office. It's almost two," she says, slipping back into her professional mode. I look at my phone, and sure enough, almost two hours have passed. How the fuck did that happen? I never lose track of time.

I clear my throat and nod, calling up my driver to pick us up since we've walked quite a few blocks away from the office. He pulls up in no time.

"I think I'll walk if that's okay," Luna says.

I won't lie, I'm disappointed that she doesn't want to ride with me, but I understand.

"That's fine. I'll see you back in the office."

She gives me a half-hearted smile and then flits away. My little hummingbird.

Chapter 8

Luna

It's been four weeks since Declan and I had our lunch date. Not that it was a date. I'm not sure what it was. We talked and he even smiled. I got to see more of the real him, the one I got a hint of during my interview.

And then there was that almost kiss. It took everything in me not to give in. His large hands holding me so close, those chiseled muscles brushing against my soft curves, the look of desire in his eyes that I've never seen before. I felt safe and secure and wanted and sexy. When he cupped my face and traced my lips, I almost lost it.

But I couldn't let anything happen. Even though every cell in my body was buzzing with desire for Declan, I couldn't be selfish. Kissing my boss is one sure way to lose this job, and that's not an option. Lucas needs treatment and stability more than I need to be kissed.

Declan has reverted back to either ignoring me or ordering me around in what I've come to understand is his signature icy tone. Others seem to jump right into action when he goes all boss mode on them, but I know better. I know he has a soft side he keeps guarded with all those walls of his. But, as I said, I still very much need this job. So I follow suit when he dishes out orders.

Today is no different. I know Declan is under a lot of stress because he's finally getting another meeting with Mr. Hashimoto. It's one that he had to work hard for after his last assistant dropped the ball big time. I think it's made him extra impatient and unreasonable with me, micromanaging my every move. It's driving me nuts, but I understand.

I've been pulling ten-hour days this last week, which makes me feel guilty for not being there while Lucas is sick. He started his second round of chemo today, and I thought for sure things would be a little more under control by now so I could get away. Unfortunately, that's not the case. Despite my long hours, it seems Declan's list of impossible demands is ever-growing. And thanks to the app I had him and the rest of his team download, I know that every single list item is "high priority." I'm really regretting that damn app right about now.

Just as I'm checking it on my phone for the tenth time today, I get a phone call. When I look at the screen, my heart catches in my throat and then plummets to my stomach. It's the hospital.

I rush out into the hallway to take the call in private.

"Hello? This is Luna Foster."

"Ms. Foster, this is Dr. Stanhope's nurse, Sandra."

"Yes, yes, what's wrong? Is Lucas okay? Did he get through his chemo appointment?" I'm trying, unsuccessfully to keep the panic out of my voice.

"He fainted about half-way through. We have him in the ICU right now, under observation. Ms. Foster, I think it's best you come down here. We're still running tests—"

"I'm on my way." I hang up without giving her the chance to finish.

Running back into the office, I don't even take time to shut down my computer or talk to anyone. I just grab my purse and coat and rush out. I can practically feel Tiffany staring daggers into my back as I storm into the elevator, but I don't have any energy left to care. I feel like I'm walking through water as I finally step into the elevator.

After the longest thirty minutes in the history of the world, I make it to the hospital. I follow some signs to the proper parking place – who knew there were so many options? I swear they built three new parking lots since the last time I was here. In a daze, I stumble into the hospital and make it to the front desk of the ICU.

"Lucas," I pant out. "Lucas Foster."

The lady at the front desk furrows her brow, but then looks up at me and must see my desperate, panicked state. She takes pity on me and gives me his room number without hesitation. I take a deep breath and brace myself for what I'm about to see. During the last year, Lucas has been in and out of the hospital dozens of times. Even though I've seen him in all states of sickness while lying in a hospital bed, I never get used to it.

Sure enough, when I open the door and see his too-skinny frame pumped fill of sedatives, I almost collapse. It never gets easier. Cancer is a fucking bitch.

I walk on unsteady legs over to his bedside and take his cold hand in mine.

"Hey, Lucas. No need to be dramatic. I'm here now," I tease, but then choke back a sob.

I look around at the monitors and grab the chart at the foot of the bed. After being in the hospital as many times as we have been this last year, I'm pretty good at understanding what all of the numbers mean. ECG reading, oxygen levels, blood pressure, PAP reading. He looks stable for now, though I know his blood pressure is low, which probably contributed to the fainting spell.

Just then, Dr. Stanhope walks in.

"Luna," he greets me. "Sorry to meet again under these circumstances."

I nod, not trusting my voice right now. He holds his hand out for the chart I've been looking over.

"We ran a full blood test, and, well..."

"Just tell me," I snap. I take a deep breath and try again. "I'm sorry. I'm stressed, but that's no reason to be rude." I run my hands through my hair, gathering it up and bringing it over my shoulder so I can twist it and nervously play with the ends.

"I understand. His white blood cells are extremely low, which could be from the treatment, but also could indicate rapid tumor growth. I've scheduled an MRI as soon as possible, but you know how these things work. It may be a few hours or even tomorrow. He's stable for now, as I'm sure you've already read in his chart."

I nod, taking it all in. Dr. Stanhope says something else, but I don't pay attention. He steps out shortly after, leaving me alone with my thoughts.

"Please, please, Lucas. You have to fight this. You have to get better, buddy. I need you," I whisper before resting my head down on his hospital bed, next to his hand.

I must have drifted off to sleep, because the next thing I know, I feel a hand on my head, patting me gently.

"Hey, Luna. Nice of you to join me." It's Lucas, his voice a little scratchy and strained.

I smile at him, flooded with relief that he's awake.

"I couldn't miss all the excitement," I tease as I grab for the water next to his bed. I help him drink it and then sit down.

"How long have I been out?" He asks.

I reach for my phone to check the time, ignoring the missed calls from work. I can't think about all of that now.

"I got the call about you fainting at two, and it's almost eight now."

"Ah, so I got a good little nap in." He tries laughing but ends up coughing. I help him sit up so he can work through it. Trying to get the focus off of him, Lucas motions towards the remote. "Think *Diners, Drive-Ins, and Dives* is on?"

I grin. "What is it with guys and that show? I don't understand. Doesn't it just make you hungry?"

"Luna, Luna, Luna," he shakes his head in mock disappointment. "If I have to explain it to you, you'd never get it. Maybe after a few more episodes, you'll learn to appreciate the genius behind Guy Fieri."

"Mmhm..." I roll my eyes.

Of course, he flips right to the channel, and it's on. It's always on, which truly boggles the mind. We fall into an all-too-familiar pattern of watching crappy tv, interrupted every once in a while, by nurses coming to check vitals. We both fall asleep with the tv still on to drown out the worries and bad dreams.

***

"Luna, earth to Luna." I feel something bounce off my forehead.

"Did you just throw a raisin at me?" I ask Lucas.

He shrugs and then grins in that mischievous way of his. It's good to see him like this. He even has a little bit of color back in his face. It's been two days since he was admitted. We moved out of the ICU last night after finally getting the results of the MRI. Sure enough, the chemo was the cause of his drop in white blood cell count, as well as his sudden drop in blood pressure, though there is still some concern over the tumor by his lungs.

Dr. Stanhope said we should stop the treatments for now, in favor of some alternative methods. All I heard was *expensive* methods, though I know none of that should matter as long as Lucas gets better.

Right on cue, Karen shows up, aka, *billing lady of doom*, which she will henceforth be known as. She and I have had several talks over the last year. She gives a brief nod to Lucas and then stares at me, knowing I'll follow.

"Luna," she starts. "I see you applied for a few of our grants that help with medical costs."

I nod my head, hoping for good news. God knows I could use some right about now.

"Unfortunately, the salary with your new job disqualifies you from receiving any financial aid."

My stomach drops. Yeah, the new job pays well, but not so well that I can just pay for tens of thousands of dollars of treatments without any sort of help. I already feel like I'm drowning, like I don't know what the fuck I'm doing with Lucas, let alone how to navigate the world of medicine and payments and loans and debts. I'm twenty, I don't know how to do any of this shit! But I can't dwell on that now. I can't think about anything. Not yet.

I see her getting ready to spew out more information that I can't handle, so I put a hand up to stop her. "Listen, *Karen*, I find it completely reprehensible that you are bugging me about payments while my brother is still in the damn hospital."

"Yes, well, that's usually not the protocol, but you have several overdue payments, and now with the lack of financial aid and the healthcare papers you filled out—"

"Are you going to kick a cancer patient out? Do you even have the power to do that?"

"Well, no, of course not."

"Then this discussion can wait. I'm tired, I'm hungry, I'm stressed out of my fucking mind, and the absolute last person I want to see in the whole world is you." Too far? Maybe. Ask me if I care right now.

Karen looks shocked, which satisfies me greatly.

"Alright then. I'll check back in a few days."

"Great," I tell her with all of the sarcasm I can muster. I take a cleansing breath and unclench my fists before walking back into Lucas' room.

"Everything okay?" He asks.

"Yeah, just some details to work through. Nothing for you to worry about."

"Luna..."

"Seriously, it'll be fine. I bet that stupid show you love is on," I try diverting attention as I sit down.

He looks wary of my response, but he lets me have this out. We settle in for another night of crappy tv.

"Psst, Luna. Luna,"

"Huh?" I snort awake, rubbing a crick in my neck from the uncomfortable chair I fell asleep in. "Are you okay? What's wrong?" I hop up, still groggy from my impromptu nap.

"I'm good, I'm fine," Lucas reassures me. "You should go home. Get an actual night of sleep instead of a few hours here and there."

"I'm not that tired," I say right as I yawn. Lucas smirks, knowing he's going to win.

"Seriously. No offense, but you smell. And you look terrible," he gives me an overly dramatic grimacing face.

"You always know just what to say to me to make me feel special," I deadpan.

He laughs. "For real, Luna. You gotta take care of yourself, too. Go home, take a shower, get some sleep. Shouldn't you check in with work? I don't want you losing your job because of me."

At his reminder, I get anxious all over again. I'm sure I've been fired, though I haven't gotten an email or a voicemail saying that yet. I know he's right. I'm exhausted. That last conversation with *billing lady of doom* drained every drop of my energy.

Lucas must sense that I'm about to give in.

"Do it, go home, on the count of five. One, two, three—"

I throw a pretzel at him, and he laughs. "Alright, alright. I'll go," I sigh dramatically.

I gather up the wrappers from the vending machine meals I've had over the last few days and dump them in the wastebasket. Right before I leave, I turn around and ask if I can get him anything.

"No! Now go before I page a nurse and have them escort you out of here for disturbing me," he jokes.

I roll my eyes and close his door.

Once in the parking lot, I search for my old car. Only, I can't find it. It's dark out now and looking at my phone I see it's almost midnight. I remember having trouble figuring out which parking lot I was supposed to go to, but I'm pretty sure I'm in the right place. I'm just turned around, that's all. I must be delusional or something from the lack of sleep.

I head back inside to the front desk. Maybe they can point me in the right direction.

"Hi, I can't seem to find my car. I parked in the blue lot. I think."

"That's short-term parking. If you've been there for more than twelve hours, your car is probably towed."

"What?"

She repeats herself and gives me the number of the towing company. I mumble out some sort of thanks, or at least I think I do. How many more hits can I take before I fall apart completely?

I start walking towards the bus stop a few blocks away. The bus only runs every few hours this late at night, but luckily there is one scheduled to come in fifteen minutes. At least one thing is going my way today. I scrounge around in my purse for bus fare. Good thing I have a few bucks left in quarters from cashing out that last twenty for coins for the vending machine.

The bus comes and I hop on, fighting sleep. My body feels like it weighs a thousand pounds, and my eyelids droop and then close. I'll just close them for a second...

"Miss? You gotta get up. It's the end of the line." A gruff voice startles me awake.

"Oh, sorry," I mumble. I gather my things and stumble out of the bus. Instead of being anywhere near my apartment, however, I'm in front of what looks to be abandoned warehouses.

"Wait!" I call out at the last minute before the bus driver closes the door. "Where am I?" I thought this was the B route to south Bronx?"

"Sorry, babe. You got the wrong bus. This is the seventeen, to Brooklyn."

"Fuck."

"I'm taking my fifteen-minute break, and then you can hop back on at the stop down the block and I can drop you off in front of the hospital," he offers. I already know I don't have enough cash for the return trip, let alone another bus back home.

"No, thanks," I wave him off.

"Suit yourself," he shrugs before closing the doors.

"Motherfucking goddamn fuck...shit!" I yell into the universe once the bus is gone.

I pull out my phone and scroll through my contacts, knowing I really only have one friend in the world. I didn't realize until just now how isolated I've let myself become. I knew my friend group had diminished – cancer has a way of weeding out your true friends, for better or worse – but I didn't notice that Sarah is the only person who even talks to me anymore. And we don't even talk that often.

I sigh and dial her number, hoping, praying, pleading with every god I can think of that she answers.

No such luck. I try again, but it goes straight to voicemail.

I'm almost at my breaking point, but I know I have to keep it together just a little bit longer. I can't break down here. I just have to get home. Scrolling through my contacts again, my thumb hovers over Declan's name. I had to get his cell phone number to add him to the project management app.

Would he answer his phone this late? Would he pick up if he saw it was me? Do I even have a job anymore? Does it matter if I can somehow get a ride home?

I shiver against the cool wind, inadvertently pressing my thumb down on Declan's name. Well, I guess the decision was made for me. Thanks, universe.

One ring.

Two rings.

Three rings.

"Luna?" His deep, silky smooth voice drifts through the phone. If I didn't know any better, I'd think there was a hint of worry in his tone. But that can't be right. It's probably annoyance.

"Hello? Luna?" He asks again.

"Hi," I squeak out. I clear my throat and try again. I need to get through this before I lose my nerve and hang up. "I parked in the blue parking lot and my car was towed and...and I'm stupid and took the wrong bus and now I'm in some abandoned warehouse in Brooklyn and I don't have enough cash to get on another bus because I spent it all in the vending machine and I just need a ride home. I'm so tired. I'm sorry, I don't have any other friends. Not that you're my friend, I just meant I don't have anyone, and I'm sorry, I just need a ride. You don't have to come; you can just send someone. You have a driver, right? I'll pay you back for his services. You can take it out of my last paycheck. I just...please? I don't have anyone else..."

I end my pathetic rant that I hope made some sort of sense.

There's silence on the other line, but I still hear him breathing. Surely, he wouldn't just leave me out here, right? He might hate me, and he'll probably fire me after this, and he's cold, but he's not heartless. I hope.

"Send me your location. I'll be there soon."

With that, he hangs up. They are the sweetest eight words I've ever heard him say to me.

Chapter 9

Declan

When my phone rang at one-thirty in the morning, I had every intention of yelling at whoever the fuck dared to wake me up at this hour. But then Luna's name flashed across the screen and panic gripped my heart for some strange reason.

I've been thinking about her more than I should, *missing* her more than I should these last three days. I finally had a reason to fire her. I think the board would agree that leaving in the middle of the workday and not coming back for days on end without any sort of communication is grounds for dismissal. But I didn't want her gone. I just wanted her back.

I tried not to worry about her, tried pushing her out of my thoughts, but how can you forget someone like Luna? I mean, shit, her desk alone is a colorful and distracting reminder of the bright and eager young woman who somehow got under my skin.

I can't count how many times I looked up from my desk these past few days, expecting to see her in some ridiculous outfit, typing away at her computer with that damn orange blanket draped over her shoulders.

And here she was, my personal temptation, the object of my inappropriate fantasies, calling me in the middle of the night.

Luna rambled on about vending machines and busses and a blue parking lot. If I didn't know any better, I'd think she was drunk. But somehow, I know she was telling the truth when she said she was exhausted. I could hear it in her voice, in her desperate tone, how she pleaded with me and told me how she had no one else. Something about that broke me deep inside. I felt an unfamiliar pain for the girl. It wasn't pity; it was a genuine heartache. It made my chest tight.

I shove those feelings aside and call up my driver. Raul seems a bit groggy but promises to be at my door in twenty minutes. I tell him

I'll pay him five-hundred dollars on the spot if he gets here in ten. I don't want Luna to be left out all alone in the cold for any longer than necessary.

She sent me her location as soon as we hung up. She is in Brooklyn, which isn't the worst part of the city, but it's still New York, which means no place is truly safe after dark. She somehow wound up in an old abandoned warehouse district, which is even less safe.

I pay Raul the five-hundred and then promise another five-hundred if he can get me to Luna's location in under twenty minutes. Normally getting to Brooklyn from my penthouse in Manhattan would take thirty minutes or more, even at this hour, but I have faith that Raul can do the impossible. That's what I expect from all of my employees.

Before long, Raul is pulling up to the curb and parking in front of a bus stop. I almost don't see Luna, but then I catch sight of the red, form-fitting slacks she was wearing the last time I saw her. She's been wearing the same outfit for three days...what the hell happened to her?

I hop out of the back seat right as Luna steps towards the car. She looks like she's been hit by a fucking semi. Her clothes are wrinkled and her hair is frazzled like she's been running her delicate fingers through it and pulling at the strands. What grips me the most, however, are her eyes. They look sunken and defeated.

We don't say anything, she just crawls into the back of the car and curls up in the seat. I follow her in and tell Raul to take us back to my place. There's no way I'm going to send her back to her place in the state she's in. Plus, I deserve answers. Luna either doesn't hear or doesn't care that I told the driver to go to my home and not hers.

Almost as soon as we drive away from the curb, Luna falls asleep. I get that tight feeling in my chest again. We take a sharp turn, and Luna leans on my shoulder, not waking up at all. I can't help myself. I gently guide her so she's laying down with her head in my lap.

Luna sniffles and her shoulders shake. I've never seen someone cry in their sleep, but here she is, curled up on my lap, sound asleep. Every few minutes she makes these heart-wrenching whimpers and her whole body trembles just once, before a few tears drip down her face onto my pants.

I'm torn between waking her up and demanding that she tells me the reason behind her tears, and just letting her sleep. Clearly, she needs it. I decide to let her rest. When I feel her tremble again, my hand moves on its own to tuck some hair behind her ear. I let my fingers linger in her soft locks, stroking her and trying to provide some comfort.

Touching her hair is like touching sunlight; bright and shiny. The texture of it somehow seeps beneath my fingertips and enters my bloodstream, causing my body to flush with heat and need. I don't think I've ever done anything like this with any of the women I've been with. This feels intimate. Tender. Not my style.

We pull into the underground parking lot of my building and I scoop Luna up in my arms, carrying her to the elevator. She snuggles up into my chest, still sound asleep. When I see her red, tear-stained face and long eyelashes wet with tears, I almost break. I almost cry right along with her at whatever brought her to this point.

Gone is the bright woman with the loud clothing. Gone is the spitfire who put me in my place and went toe to toe with me about that project management app that actually has made my life a lot easier. Gone is the animated, lively woman who unashamedly ate six tacos and made me smile at her endless stories. Right now, I'm looking at the ghost of Luna, and it honestly scares the shit out of me. I want nothing more than to bring back my hummingbird.

We make it to my penthouse, and I carry her to the guest room, laying her down on the bed once I've pulled the covers down. Carefully, I slip her heels off and remove her jacket. I want to strip her down completely, though I chastise myself for having those kinds of thoughts during this situation. I can't seem to help it. Everything about Luna calls to me.

Fuck, I could have lost her. The thought slams into me so hard I find it difficult to breathe. I didn't realize how important Luna had become to me these last few weeks, but knowing I have her here with me, safe and sound, brings a peace I didn't know I had been missing.

I pull the blankets over her tiny, shivering frame and tuck her wild blonde hair behind her ear. She blinks awake and looks at me, the absolute picture of exhaustion.

"Declan?" She whispers.

"Shh, get some rest now, Luna."

Unable to keep her eyes open any longer, she simply nods and snuggles down into the bed. I watch her for far too long, aching with the need to kiss her forehead and crawl into bed with her so I can hold her tight and take away her pain.

Eventually, I leave her be, though each step away from her, away from my broken, vulnerable little Luna, is painful. I don't understand what she's done to me, how she's brought out these feelings of protectiveness, possessiveness, and longing, but they are coursing through my veins, slowly penetrating my cold heart and replacing indifference with the need to take care of her.

I strip down and throw on a pair of pajama pants before crawling into my own bed. I go to sleep with thoughts of Luna. One thought, really. *Mine.*

Chapter 10

I roll over on what is possibly the softest mattress I've ever slept on, which is weird. I should be at the hospital. I should be on the scratchy cot or the broken rocker that won't recline.

Instead, I'm warm and cozy and well-rested. My back doesn't hurt, my neck doesn't hurt, my eyes don't feel dried out and irritated. I can't bring myself to actually open them yet, in case this is all a dream.

Curiosity wins out, and I open one eye, then the other. I'm greeted with a pure white bed and down comforter, as well as a stack of pillows I'm all curled up around. I sit up and look around the room.

There's a huge oak wardrobe with a matching dresser and vanity, as well as a few paintings that look abstract and expensive. This is by far the fanciest, most elegant room I've ever seen, let alone stepped into. It's not an over-the-top showing of wealth. In fact, the whole room screams minimal, but each piece of furniture is undoubtedly worth more than six months' worth of my rent. I swing my legs over the bed and sink my toes into the softest, fluffiest rug. It, too, it white.

On the nightstand next to me, I see a note in familiar handwriting. It's then I remember last night. I was a complete wreck. A wrung-out, disaster of a hot mess. And I called Declan.

Oh my God.

I called Declan. I vaguely remember rambling on about the bus and not having anyone else. Pathetic. God, I'm so pathetic. And I had to have been gross. Shit, I'm still gross. I shouldn't care about what he thinks of me as long as he got me out of that scary warehouse, but I do.

I sigh and rub a hand down my greasy, puffy face. I take a few deep breaths. What's done is done. I need to be an adult and thank Declan for picking me up, and then I'll shamefully ask him for a few bucks so I can call a cab. Like the absolute pitiful person that I am.

I grab the note, half expecting it to say something about leaving as soon as possible. Instead, what I read almost brings tears to my eyes.

Luna,

I hope you slept well. There's a bathroom across the hall, please feel free to shower or take a bath. You should find everything you need in there. When you are ready, there is breakfast waiting in the kitchen.

Yours,

Declan

"Mine?" I whisper. The sentiment makes my insides all mushy. He probably doesn't mean anything by it. Then again, Declan has never been one much for saying things he doesn't mean.

I contemplate a bath, but in the end I opt for a shower. Not that that's much of a sacrifice. The shower is huge, with a see-through glass door and one of those shower heads with a hundred different settings. Just like Declan said, there's everything I need, including lemon lavender shampoo, conditioner, and a fresh bar of soap still in the wrapper with some fancy French name on the front.

Twenty minutes later, I feel like a new person. There was a bottle of fancy French lotion to match the soap sitting on the marble counter, so I helped myself to that as well. I swear I'm glowing, and my hair has never been this soft.

I'm a little self-conscious about wearing the clothes Declan left folded up on the counter next to the lotion – a pair of his boxers and a t-shirt – but I can't very well put on the clothes I came here in. Not after the most luxurious shower of my life.

I tiptoe down the hall, feeling completely out of place. This is my *boss*'s home. I shouldn't even *be* here, let alone shower and wear his clothes. It all feels so...intimate. Familiar. Like we're lovers.

That thought has my cheeks burning red, and my pussy shamefully wet. I take a deep breath and get myself under control. This doesn't mean anything. Declan probably felt bad for me. I mean, I was in rough shape last night. Who knows what he thinks about me or what I've been up to the last few days.

I make it to the kitchen and see a tray of fresh fruit, a dozen pastries, a pitcher of orange juice that I just know is fresh-squeezed, and a carafe of coffee. There's a plate, napkin, silverware, and a mug set up for me at the breakfast bar.

Never one to turn down a free meal, especially these days, I grab a croissant and an apple turnover and pile on strawberries and grapes. I also grab an orange for good measure. Vitamin C and all that. I pour myself a steaming cup of coffee and close my eyes, just breathing in the earthy, delicious scent. It has nothing on the crappy hospital coffee, that's for sure.

Without further ado, I devour the apple turnover. I'm half-way through demolishing the croissant when I hear a familiar voice.

"Morning, Luna," Declan says, his deep timbre rolling through me and setting my nerves on fire.

I look up from my plate and see my boss standing in front of me. Only, he doesn't look like my boss. No, today Declan has on joggers that hang low on his hips and a white t-shirt stretched over his broad chest. I knew he was toned and epically gorgeous underneath his suit, but I never had proof until this moment. And fuck, is he gorgeous. Not just those strong arms and sculpted pecs I can see with his shirt stretched so tight, but his face. It looks different. Softer.

"Hi," I squeak out.

Declan grins at me. Like, actually grins. It's my new favorite look and I'm sure I'll be thinking of it later tonight when I'm back in my lumpy bed, with my hand between my legs, like I've been doing for the last month.

To my absolute shock, he closes the distance between us and leans over the breakfast bar. I think he's about to kiss me, but then I feel his thumb wipe away some crumbs from my face. I should be embarrassed, but the gesture is uncharacteristically sweet of him. Plus, he's giving me this soft smile, like he enjoyed touching me very much. God knows I did.

"Are you feeling better this morning. Or, this afternoon, rather?"

My eyebrows lift up in shock. "This afternoon?"

"It's almost twelve-thirty."

"Oh my God, I'm so sorry. I didn't mean to sleep that late, I guess I just—"

"You needed it," he says, cutting me off from my rambling apology. "No need to apologize, little Luna."

Little Luna. How many times have I pictured him calling me that while pleasuring myself? He said it that day we almost kissed. *What are you doing to me, little Luna?*

The endearment has me blushing again. I dip my head down so he doesn't see it. Again, to my shock, Declan places his forefinger underneath my chin and tips my face up towards his.

"You didn't answer my question. Are you feeling better?"

"Much," I all but whisper. I clear my throat and try again. "Thank you. For picking me up and letting me stay here. I'll get out of here as soon as possible."

"No," he barks. His tone is harsh, much like he is when he's at the office. "Sorry," he says more gently. "I just mean, you can't leave in my boxers, right?"

There's that grin again. And is that a dimple? *Fuck. Me.* Seriously.

"Um, right. I can...I'll go change..."

"Luna, relax. I brought you here. I want you here."

My brow furrows in confusion. "You do? Aren't you pissed at me for blowing off work?"

"I was, yes," he answers on a sigh. "But then I was just worried. And when you called me in the middle of the night—"

"I'm sorry about that, I just—"

He puts a hand up to stop me.

"When you called me, I panicked. And when I found you..." Declan looks at me with such sadness and is that concern is his beautiful gray eyes? "Where have you been?" He asks as he walks around the breakfast bar and sits on the stool next to me.

I push the tray of pastries over to him, hoping to distract him with breakfast so I don't have to answer. He declines the food, saying he doesn't much care for sweets. Weirdo.

"My brother, Lucas, he's sick. Lymphoma," I start. "I told you my mom died last year? Well, Lucas was just sixteen at the time, so I became his legal guardian. And its' been...well, it's been difficult. I dropped out of school and got a job as a waitress—" I clap my hand over my mouth, realizing what I just told him.

I venture a look up at Declan, expecting him to be angry with me for lying on my resume. Instead, I look up and see that grin on his face. He's chuckling and shaking his head.

"You're the best damn assistant I've ever had and you haven't even graduated college," he chuckles again. "I figured you were dishonest on your resume, but truthfully, I don't even care. You're good at your job, Luna. I know I've never said that before, but it's true."

I have to look away from him. It's too much, his praise, his attention. But then his words sink in. I take a chance and blurt out what I'm thinking before I can chicken out.

"Does that mean I still have a job?" I hold my breath as I wait for his answer.

"Yes, little Luna. You have a job as long as you want. But you have to communicate with me. Tell me things, okay? I didn't know about your brother."

"I didn't think you'd care," I say, continuing on in my boldness now that I know I have a job.

"You're right, or at least, that's been true in the past. I never gave a shit about my employees' personal lives. But you..." He shakes his head again, almost like he can't believe what he's going to say next. "You changed me. I care. I care about you."

His words and sincerity have me tearing up. Who is this man sitting next to me? Does Declan have a twin brother? Is this their thing - switching places and confusing the crap out of people?

He reaches out and wipes away the single tear that escaped with the back of his knuckle.

"Now, tell me the rest. Why did you leave so suddenly?"

I take a deep breath and continue my explanation. "Lucas was starting his second round of chemo and fainted. The hospital called, and I panicked. I rushed over there to be with him. We're all each other has, you know? They ran all sorts of tests, and to be honest, one day sort of bled into the next. When you're in the hospital and grabbing a few hours of sleep here and there, it's hard to tell if you've been there a day or a year."

Declan nods, encouraging me to go on.

"It wasn't until Lucas told me I looked like a hot mess and needed a shower that I finally agreed to go home. But my car was towed, and it was the middle of the night and I only had enough money for one bus ride. Then I stupidly hopped on the wrong bus and...well, you know the rest."

"How is Lucas now?" It warms my heart that his first question is about Lucas.

"He's stable. Doing better. They are stopping his chemo and trying to get me to agree to some alternative treatments."

"Why haven't you moved forward with that?"

"Just some details to work out," I tell him, hoping my voice comes across as casual. The last person in the world I want to know about all of the debt I'm in is Declan.

He looks like he wants to say something but decides against it.

We sit in silence for a few moments, and then I try to break the awkwardness. "I should be getting back. Wait, you said it's already afternoon? What about work?"

"I took the day off," he shrugs.

"You...took the day off?" I can hardly believe it. He took the day off because of me?

"Sure. I can't get anything done without my assistant anyway," he teases. I'd feel bad about that, but the smile on his face says he didn't mean it as an insult.

Whatever is happening between us is confusing and I'm feeling even more vulnerable sitting here in Declan's clothes. I gather up my dishes and make my way to the sink to begin washing them.

I feel Declan's body heat behind me, and I gasp a little bit. I turn around, but he's much closer than I thought. I'm knocked off balance, but Declan reaches out with one hand on my lower back and pulls me into his hard chest. It's so much like that day all those weeks ago, my body pressed against his, my breath uneven and shallow, my heart pounding around in my ribcage.

His other hand comes up to wrap around the side of my neck, his thumb grazing my jaw. Declan's gray eyes roam over my face, taking in every inch of me. I feel exposed but safe. Broken open, but truly seen for the first time in so long.

"I'm going to kiss you now, my little Luna," Declan whispers, his warm breath teasing across my face and making me so, so wet.

I nod and part my lips for him, though my mind is racing with a million different thoughts. What about Lucas? What if this ends badly? What if we end up in bed together? What if I'm no good? What if he wants someone more experienced?

His mouth meets mine and the whole world stops.

Chapter 11

Declan

Her taste wrecks me.

She's sweet and citrusy, but there's something there that's just...Luna.

She parts those precious lips of hers and lets me in, lets me drink more of her down, lets me become completely addicted to her. Never, in all my years, has one kiss so completely destroyed me.

And then she moans.

Softly at first, like she doesn't know if she should. Our tongues tangle as my hands slide up and down her body, over the curve of her breast, her ribcage, her small waist, finally landing on her hips. I pull her towards me and slide my hands lower to her thighs, lifting Luna up onto the counter in one swift move, my mouth never leaving hers. She moans loudly as we both get completely lost in this kiss.

I already know it won't be our last. No fucking way.

I need more, need to feel her skin under my tongue, need to lap at those perky nipples, need to breathe her in. I need to see her cum. I need to smell her release as it drips down my chin.

Reluctantly, I break our kiss so I can fill my lungs with air. She follows me like our lips are connected by magnets. It pleases me to know she's as addicted to me as I already am to her.

I watch as she catches her breath, her eyes closed, lips swollen, cheeks flushed.

"Beautiful," I whisper into the side of her neck before placing a soft kiss there.

I feel her pulse beating rapidly, which makes me groan and lick the same spot. She bucks her hips, grazing her hot little pussy against me.

"Do you like when I kiss you here, little Luna?" I ask as I continue trailing kisses up and down her slender column.

"Yes...sir," she whimpers.

I growl into her skin, my already hard dick becoming granite at her words. She tilts her neck, baring the soft flesh to me. I feel like a wolf, needing to sink my teeth into my prey.

"Fucking love when you call me that," I growl again, sucking and licking and nipping as she moans for me.

My lips trail lower, grazing her collarbone, where I suck and bite her, just enough to turn her skin pink, not enough to leave a mark. But fuck, I want to mark her. Claim her. Devour her.

"Please," Luna whimpers again as I slowly kiss my way down her chest, over the fabric of the shirt she's wearing. "I need more. Please, Declan."

"Who?" I ask, before rolling her nipple in between my lips.

"Sir! Oh, fuck, please, sir!"

I reward her by sucking her breast into my mouth and slipping my hands under her shirt, exploring her silky-smooth skin. My large hands skim up her soft tummy, higher, higher, till my thumbs graze the sensitive underside of her breasts.

Luna lifts her arms up, giving me the green light to take her shirt off. I grip the hem of the too-large shirt and slowly slide it up her body, revealing inch after creamy inch of skin to my hungry eyes.

I stop when the hem of the shirt is just below her tits and look up at Luna. She bites her bottom lip and looks at me with equal parts excitement and apprehension. I lean down and kiss her softly, sensing she needs this from me too.

"You're so beautiful, Luna. You're perfect," I whisper into her lips before kissing her again.

She opens her eyes, and all hesitation is gone, replaced by a playful twinkle. Jesus Christ, what that does to me.

"How do you know? You haven't even seen everything yet."

There's that spark. I missed it. I needed to see it after the way she cried in my arms last night.

"Well let's see what we can do to fix that, shall we?"

I practically tear the shirt off of her, and then stand back and admire the most perfect pair of tits I've ever seen.

"Fucking hell," I whisper. I brush the back of my knuckles down the top of one breast and over the pebbled little nipple, loving the way she trembles at my touch.

Leaning down, I lick over her aching peaks before blowing cold air on them. Luna gasps as her thighs tighten around my waist. I suck on her breast, *hard*, loving the way her body fits so perfectly with mine. I caress her thighs as I suck and nibble one breast and then the other. She leans back with her hands on the counter, thrusting her chest out for me and pushing her breast deeper into my mouth.

I groan at her offering and then pop off her tit only to repeat the process on the other one. The whole time, my thumbs massage circles on the insides of Luna's thighs, inching higher and higher.

"Oh, God, ohmygod, I..."

"Shit, are you going to cum for me right now?"

She cries out as I pull her nipple through my teeth, her legs shaking, her heart pounding in her chest. I feel the heat of her pussy as she grinds down against my throbbing cock, seeking the friction she needs.

"I think...I think..."

My hands slide around to her back, holding her up just as her arms give out. Luna throws her head back in a silent scream as I bite her nipple. I watch in complete awe as this goddess cums in my arms. I feel every muscle in her back tense and release as I hold her close and kiss all over her breasts and neck.

Finally, Luna goes limp in my arms. I gather her up and hold her close to my chest, kissing the top of her head.

"Goddamn, Luna, I've never seen someone cum just from playing with their tits."

She looks up at me and blushes but then buries her head in my chest again.

"Sorry," she whispers. "Is that bad?"

"No, it's fucking hot. What kind of men have you been with?" I meant it as a joke, but now I don't want to know. I don't want to hear about her and other men.

When she goes stiff in my arms, however, I lean back a bit and tilt her chin up.

"Luna?"

She avoids eye contact. "No one," she whispers. I almost don't hear it.

"What?"

"There haven't been...I mean, I'm still..."

She hides her face in her hands while I'm still trying to figure out if I'm understanding her correctly. I peel away one small hand and then the other, placing a kiss on both palms and then wrapping them around my neck.

I rest my forehead on hers and breathe her in.

"Are you telling me you're a virgin, sweetheart?"

"Yes, sir," she whispers. Luna bites that damn lip of hers and I can't help but take her lips in a possessive kiss.

"Jesus, Luna," I growl before diving in again. "Am I the first to see these tits of yours too?"

She nods.

"Need your words."

"Yes, sir."

I grunt in approval and I kiss my way down her neck, her chest until I'm nuzzling between her perfect mounds.

And then I kiss lower.

My lips trail over her ribcage, her tummy, as I gently lay her out on the counter and kneel down in front of her.

"Am I going to be the first to lick your dripping pussy? The first to taste you and suck on your needy little clit?"

Luna moans as I hook my thumbs in the waistband of the boxers she's wearing. I pause until I hear her say it.

"Yes, sir, only you."

I slide the boxers off of her and trail kisses up the inside of one thigh and then the other. I stroke my fingers through the soft patch of curls decorating her mound, and grin when she shivers and squirms.

"And will I be the first one to dip my fingers into your tight little cunt?"

"Yes!"

I smack her pussy, not too hard, and Luna spasms and gasps in surprise.

"Yes, who?"

She's panting now, her fingers gripping the side of the counter so hard her knuckles are white.

I smack her cunt again and watch it twitch, a pool of her juices gathering on the table. Fucking hell, she's perfect.

"Fuck, yes, sir. Sir, please," she whimpers.

"Love when you beg so nicely for me, little Luna," I growl as I throw her legs over my shoulders. I part her lips with my thumbs and stare at the most decadent pussy I've ever seen. She's absolutely soaking wet and I can see her clit, engorged and throbbing for me. Precum leaks out of my aching cock as I let her scent wash over me.

I feel her body shaking in my hands, vibrating with so much need and anticipation. I blow warm air over her tight cunt and watch it convulse for me, a wave of wetness gushing from her virgin hole. One drop of honey trickles down to her puckered little asshole and I lick it up, not stopping until I circle her clit with the tip of my tongue.

"Declan! Sir!" Her voice cracks as she gasps for air.

God, her sounds, the way she says my name, calls me sir...fuck, it makes my cock throb and my balls ache. How can she unravel me with just that small thing?

"Say it again," I demand.

"Declan...*sir*," she moans. "I like the way that feels."

"Good," I murmur. "I like the way it makes you say my name."

I lap at her sweet pussy, spearing my tongue inside of her entrance and scooping up more of her juices to swirl around her clit. Luna's hips buck against me, her thighs tighten around my head, and I can tell she's going to cum again.

But I want to drag it out more.

I look up from between her legs and watch her tits rise and fall as she pants for air. Jesus, the sight alone has me spurting more precum into my pants. She's captivating, every single thing about her.

I slowly lick at the seam where her leg meets her hip, first one, and then the other. I trace around the outside of her pussy lips, and then dart my tongue into her slit, licking her clit just once. She twists, and I move my tongue back to doing lazy circles around her folds and dips. I repeat this process, torturing her, bringing her closer and closer just one lick at a time.

Sucking her clit into my mouth, I swipe my tongue over the tight bundle of nerves again and again until I feel her muscles pull tight, her breath catching in her throat and then...

I back away, grinning when I hear her frustrated grunt.

"I need to cum!"

"Trust me, my little hummingbird. I'll make it worth the wait."

I play with Luna some more, swiping a finger up and down her pussy, chuckling when her greedy cunt tries to suck me inside.

"Love how responsive you are. So fucking sexy." I tell her right before plunging my first finger inside of her.

"Oh!" Her surprised little yelp turns into a moan as I pump in and out. "More!"

I withdraw my finger and smack her clit, making her gush for me and cry out. I plunge two fingers in her tight channel, in and out, curling them up and rubbing them over her G-spot. I take them out just as quickly and smack her pussy again.

"How do good girls ask for what they want?"

"More, sir, make me fucking cum, please, please..."

I growl in approval and shove three fingers inside of her dripping pussy while biting down on her clit. Luna bows her back off of the kitchen counter, every single muscle in her body drawn up tight. Then she jerks her hips up and thrashes underneath me, so much so that I have to keep my other hand over her stomach to keep her from falling off the damn counter.

I keep fingerfucking her as her pussy squeezes me tightly, my thumb taking the place of my mouth so I can watch her tiny body get overtaken by pleasure. When Luna gasps for air, I can tell she thinks it's over.

But I keep going. I curl my fingers up again and again while keeping her pinned to the counter. I feel it, I feel her orgasm deep in her bones. I feel it rising to the surface as I beckon it with my hand deep inside her cunt, fingers smacking with each thrust.

"Declan, I'm..."

"Let it happen, Luna. Let go for me."

"Ah, ah, ah, oh fuck, ohmygod, there, right there..."

Luna screams and shatters so beautifully for me. I withdraw my hand and bury my face in her legs, gripping her ass in my hands and bringing her closer to me so I can drink down all of her release. I can't even breathe, but I don't give a fuck. She's exquisite.

"Too...much..." She tries to twist out of my grip, but I snarl at her like the feral beast she makes me. I lick that pussy clean and feel the final tremors of her orgasms leave her in a shuddering breath.

I stand and scoop Luna's tiny, limp body up in my arms and sit us down on the couch, with her curled up in my lap. It's a special kind of hell having the sexiest woman I've ever seen, completely naked on my lap while my cock is aching and harder than it's ever been, but this wasn't about that. Her pleasure will always come first.

I cup her head with one hand and tuck her into my chest, while stroking her bare back with my other hand, hoping to provide some comfort to her after such an intense first sexual experience.

"You did so good, my little hummingbird. You're so beautiful, letting me have control of your pleasure like that," I whisper before kissing the top of her head. "Are you okay, sweetheart?"

Luna takes a stuttering breath, and for a moment I worry that I pushed her too far. I mean, I did just give her three orgasms. And she's so small and inexperienced. I lost control once I had a taste of her sweet honey. Which is not something I do. I am in control, always. Even of my own pleasure. But this woman in my arms... She breaks me and rattles me and terrifies me and confuses me. And I want more.

"I've never felt...I didn't know..." She sighs. "I'm so good, Declan. I mean, sir."

I chuckle and kiss the top of her head again.

"You can call me Declan. Sir is just when we play, do you understand?"

She nods into my chest.

"Need your words, Luna."

"I understand."

"Good girl. My beautiful hummingbird," I praise.

"Why do you call me that?"

I smile, thinking about the first time I called her *hummingbird* all those weeks ago.

"That's what you are. Tiny, colorful, beautiful. Delicate but strong. Always moving around and fixing things."

"And I love sugar?" She pops her little head up and smiles at me. Fuck, my chest hurts with how adorable and beautiful and *mine* she is.

"That's something we have in common then. An appreciation for fine desserts."

"What? I thought you said you weren't a big fan of sweets!"

I give a devious grin. "That's not the kind of dessert I was thinking about..."

"Oh my God!" She giggles, blushing furiously.

I can't help it. I have to kiss her.

So, I do.

When we come up for air, I rest my forehead on hers.

"I can't believe this is really happening," she whispers after a few beats of silence.

"And what's that?"

"Uh, I mean, not that anything is *happening* or that like we're *together* or whatever."

I should have mercy on her, but it's just too fun to watch her squirm.

"Luna," I finally say after she's ended her little outburst. "I just gave you three orgasms, and I plan on giving you many more. As much as your little body can handle. And then some."

She smiles, but I can tell she's still tense. She won't meet my gaze. I take a deep breath and say something I never thought I'd say to anyone.

"Look at me, little hummingbird." I cup her face and turn her towards me. "We're together, you and me. You've gotten under my skin and I'm not ready to let you go."

This seems to satisfy her. I press a soft kiss to her forehead, knowing that what I'm feeling is so much more than just her getting under my skin. She cracked my damn heart wide open and replaced all the cold, broken parts with her light and warmth. I don't know that I'd survive it if she walked away, which is crazy. It's too much. It's too scary for her to hear right now. Or maybe it's too scary for me to voice.

I look down and see my little Luna sleeping in my arms, which makes me chuckle. How things have changed in just a day.

Chapter 12

Luna

I wake up to soft, teasing kisses all over my face. It makes me giggle and try to get away from Declan. My boss. My boss who I thought was so cold and cruel. But here he is, being sweet and playful. What a difference just one day has made.

Finally opening my eyes, I see this beautiful, strong man smiling down at me. There's something in his gaze that's different. Not just the warmth I see there, or the hint of lust from our time together earlier, but something...I don't know. I can't quite place it. But it's there, nonetheless, and I feel it deep down inside of me.

"Come on, little hummingbird," he says in that deep voice of his I've grown to love. It used to make me break out in goosebumps from pure lust, even when he was being a jerk to me, but now it comforts me as well. I smile at his endearment for me. I like it. A lot. "I want to take advantage of my day off. Let's go do something fun."

"I never thought I'd hear those words come out of your mouth," I grin up at him.

"Yes, well, you make me say all sorts of things I've never said before, it seems."

My smile softens, thinking of all of the sweet things he's said to me today. Such a different man than I've experienced in the past.

"I should probably figure out how to get my car back from the impound lot," I sigh.

"Already taken care of."

"Huh?"

"I already paid for it. I grabbed your keys, I hope you don't mind, and had it dropped off at your place."

"I..." I don't even know what to say to all of that. "How did you know where I live?"

"Employee records," he shrugs.

"Oh, yeah. Well, thank you. I'll pay you back, I promise. How much was it?" I brace myself to hear the damage. Probably at least a few hundred dollars since it's been there several days.

"No need to pay me back. It's not a big deal."

I bristle at that. It might not be a big deal to him, but it is to me. "I don't take handouts. You're not my...my...sugar daddy. Just because we've been intimate, doesn't mean you have to pay for things." I start to get up out of his lap, but Declan won't let me go.

"Luna, that's not the kind of relationship we have, I promise you. Just let me do this."

"I don't like being indebted to others."

"And I already told you, I don't want your money."

"Right, but I'm sure you're thinking of *other* ways for me to pay you back," I snap at him.

In a flash, Declan has me on my back on the seat of the couch while he pins my naked body down with his fully clothed one.

"Enough," he says, his voice deep and commanding, even a little harsh. "I don't coerce people into having sex with me, and everything you and I do will always be consensual. I don't like your accusations, and I don't like the fact that you're lowering yourself to that."

I feel stupid tears burn in my eyes and I try to look away from him. I don't even know why I'm crying.

Declan kisses my temple and rests his forehead on mine.

"Let me do this for you. I promise I don't want anything in return," he says, his voice softer, almost pleading with me.

"Fine. For now. But we're not done talking about this." I try to make my tone firm, but even I can hear how weak I sound. Declan smiles and gives me a chaste kiss before helping me stand up.

"Go on, little hummingbird. I want to take you to one of my favorite places in the city," he says, swatting my ass as I take a step away from him, making me jump.

"As long as it isn't another French restaurant," I tease. He spanks me again, which actually makes me gasp and my pussy clench. I mean, what the hell is wrong with me?

Declan gets that dark look in his eyes, the same one he had before he buried his head between my thighs and made me see God. "We better get going," he growls. "Before I corrupt you completely, my sweet little Luna."

I can't help the moan that escapes my throat.

"You're not ready for me yet, little girl, so don't tempt me. I'm already hard as a fucking rock and hanging on by a thread."

I hesitate for a moment, debating whether I want to push him over the edge or listen to his warning. In the end, I make my way back to the guest bedroom. He's right, I don't think I'm ready for all of him yet. But soon, I hope.

I find my clothes from yesterday washed and folded on the already made bed, which means there was a housekeeper of sorts that worked their magic while Declan and I were...indisposed. My cheeks flush with embarrassment, but also arousal. I don't hate the idea of someone else hearing what Declan did to me. What I let him do. God, this man is turning me into a sex addict, and I haven't even had sex yet!

Twenty minutes later, Declan and I are in the backseat of his car, with the driver headed off to whatever surprise location Declan has in mind. He placed his large hand over my thigh as soon as he slipped into the backseat next to me, and he hasn't moved it since. It's part sweet and part possessive. I don't mind the gesture, though coming from anyone else I'd have yanked my leg away in a heartbeat.

Declan is looking out of his window, which allows me the opportunity to study him. He's wearing tight jeans that fit him just right, a long-sleeved Henley, and a leather jacket. I've never seen him in jeans, and fuck, is it hot. I love him in a suit, of course, but his casual look is just as devastating to my lady parts.

"You gotta stop looking at me like that, hummingbird," Declan says, his voice low and gravelly.

I snap my head to the side to look out of my window. "Like what?"

His hand shifts up my leg and Declan tightens his grip. I feel his warm breath on my neck before his lips brush against the shell of my ear.

"Like you want me to fuck you right here in the backseat of this car," he whispers.

My heart is pounding out of my chest. "How... how did you know I was looking at you?" I still refuse to turn my head to look him in the eyes.

"I could feel you undressing me with your eyes, little Luna."

I don't know what it is about him that makes me feel so bold, but before I know it, the words are tumbling out of my mouth. "It's only fair. You got to see all of me, but I haven't seen hardly any of you yet, *sir.*"

Declan groans and kisses the side of my neck, causing me to gasp. "Fuck, what you do to me..." He nips my skin and kisses the same spot, and then pulls away from me, leaving me panting and needy.

I'd think he was completely unaffected, but I see the evidence of his arousal in those tight-fitting jeans of his. Declan goes back to looking out his window, but he has a little grin on his face.

The car comes to a stop a few minutes later, in front of what appears to be an old, abandoned apartment complex. Several abandoned apartment complexes, actually. I look over at Declan with one eyebrow raised. He smirks at me and grabs my hand, pulling me out of the car with him.

Declan laces our fingers together as we walk in between two of the buildings, following an overgrown pathway. It opens up into a garden, complete with a pond. The vegetation is overgrown and clearly hasn't been tended to in quite some time, but that actually makes it all the more beautiful. Magical, even.

Since it's autumn, the few trees in the little clearing are beautiful shades of red, orange, and yellow, and the plants are still green, a few even in bloom. The pond is surprisingly clean and clear.

"It's amazing," I say reverently, not wanting to disturb the peace of the garden. "How did you find this? Why is no one else here?"

"My family used to live a few blocks away. I'd go on walks sometimes as a kid, it helped me...calm down, I guess. I stumbled upon this graveyard of buildings one day and still come back here when I need to think. I bought it years ago, but never told anyone. I haven't done anything to the buildings or the garden. I want to preserve it, keep it just like this. My little escape."

I turn my head to look at him, though he's not looking at me. Instead, he's wistfully taking in his surroundings. I look on with him, trying to picture Declan coming here as a kid. I wonder what growing up was like for him. Did he need to escape a lot?

I feel Declan step closer to me, wrapping his arms around my waist from behind. He pulls me into his chest and kisses the top of my head before resting his chin there. I love that he's so much taller than me. It makes me feel safe in his arms, surrounded by his warmth. I sigh and snuggle deeper into him.

"What do you usually come here to think about?" I ask.

He doesn't answer at first, but then he takes a deep breath and blows it out. "Work, I suppose. Or, rather, family and work. And my dad."

"He passed away recently, right?"

"Yeah. Our relationship was complicated. I think he loved us, my brothers and me. But he could be cruel. Manipulative. Every gift or gracious gesture came with strings. Sometimes it was to humiliate us, sometimes it was a power play. Like the company, for example. He passed it on to my brothers and me, on the condition that we increase profits by twenty percent in the first year and get the approval of the board. Of course, he made sure the board was composed of people loyal to him who think we didn't work for our positions. It felt like a final fuck you to Asher, Cooper, and me."

"Why don't you guys quit? Start your own company? Surely you have the money and contacts to build something of your own."

Declan sighs. "We could, and we have considered it. I guess in some messed-up way, we want to prove him wrong. Or at least, I know I do. I don't want him to win. It's stupid, I mean he's dead so he can't see whether he got to us or not, but the thought is still there. I don't know."

I turn in Declan's embrace and hug him, wrapping my arms around his torso. He seems shocked for a second, but then he returns my hug and squeezes me tightly.

Leaning back a bit, I look him in the eyes. I see such conflict there, the war inside of him clearly still tearing him apart.

"It's not stupid to want your dad to be proud of you."

His brow furrows and he opens his mouth to say something, but then shuts it again. I swear I see his eyes shining with tears, but before I can say anything, he leans down and kisses me. It's tentative, slow at first, so different than the way he devoured me earlier. One sweet kiss rolls into another, another, another until we're gasping for air as we pull apart.

"You're wise beyond your years, little Luna."

"Spoken like an old man," I tease.

He smiles, but then gets a serious look on his face. "I'm fifteen years older than you. Does that bother you?"

I didn't know how old he was, exactly, though I figured he was in his thirties.

"No. It makes me feel...I don't know. Safe. Special."

"You are those things. And so much more."

"Does our age difference bother you?"

He shakes his head. "Maybe at first. But only because I felt like a dirty old man having all of these thoughts about you," he grins.

"But you don't feel like a dirty old man anymore?" I return his grin.

"Oh, I definitely do. But I think you like it." With that, he nibbles my ear, which makes me giggle and squirm away from him.

Declan lets me go but takes my hand and leads us around the pond. I keep stealing glances at him, trying to figure out who this man is and how he seemed to change overnight.

Eventually, we head back to the car. Declan tells the driver to go back to his penthouse, but I speak up.

"Wait, I really need to get back to my place. I should change and catch up on all the chores I've been neglecting while I was at the hospital, and then I need to go visit Lucas." I glance over at Declan, who looks like he's about to object. "Before you say anything, I don't need your permission. You can't boss me around outside of work."

His stern expression turns slightly devious as he leans in to whisper into my ear. "I can boss you around anywhere, sweetheart. And I think you'll like it."

"Nope," I say, unconvincingly.

He smirks at me. "I can," he tells me in that commanding tone of his. "But I also want to take care of you. If you need to go back to your place, I'll allow it. But I'm picking you up tonight. We're going on a date. And make sure to pack your overnight bag, you'll be staying with me this weekend."

I huff out an indignant breath, though I can't deny the spark of arousal shooting through my body at the way he gives me orders. He grins like he knows exactly what he's doing to me. Declan gives the driver my address and slips his hand over my thigh again.

When we get to my apartment, Declan eyes it skeptically.

"You live here?"

Shame floods through me, but then it's replaced by anger. "What? Not up to your standards?"

"Hey now," he says gently, taking my hand in his. "That's not what I meant. I just worry about you and Lucas' safety. It doesn't look very secure."

I shrug and pull my hand out of his, unbuckling my seatbelt and getting ready to hop out of the vehicle. Instead, Declan wraps an arm around my waist and pulls me into his side. I refuse to look at him.

"I just want what's best for you, little hummingbird."

I look over my shoulder and see only sincerity in his eyes. I'm not sure what to make of his comment, so I just nod. He lets me go and follows me out before grabbing me and kissing me fiercely.

"Tonight," he growls into my lips. "Six-thirty. Remember your overnight bag."

I try to fight a smile but lose the battle in the end. I turn around to walk towards my building when I feel him smack my ass. I jump and look back at him, biting my lip. "I'll be ready, sir."

I hear him curse under his breath and then the car door slams shut.

Giggling to myself, I head inside to change my clothes and go see Lucas.

***

At six-thirty, sharp, there's a knock on my door. I smooth out the bright pink dress I'm wearing. It has a sweetheart neckline and a fitted bodice. The skirt flares out and hits mid-thigh. Since it's a bit chilly out, I pair it with thick purple tights. I complete the look with bright blue flats. I considered going with something tamer but fuck it. He knows what he's getting into, no use in hiding it now.

I open the door and see Declan in Chinos and a white t-shirt, stretched deliciously over his muscled chest. He grins at me and pulls me in for a kiss.

"Missed your colors, hummingbird," he says before nuzzling my neck.

We break apart and he grabs my duffle bag in one hand, and laces our fingers together with his other hand, tugging me along to his car.

"Where are we going?" I ask once we're inside.

"You'll just have to wait and see."

I pout, and Declan leans over to pull my bottom lip through his teeth. "You'll like it," he whispers against my lips. He gives me a chaste kiss and then sits back in his seat.

A few minutes later, the car pulls up to the curb, right in front of a closed-off street with dozens of food trucks. My eyes just about bug out of my head and I can't help but jump in excitement.

"You're voluntarily eating food from a truck?!"

"I think I'd do just about anything to see you this happy," he replies. "Besides, you were right about those tacos being delicious."

"*And* you're admitting that I was right about something?" I ask, raising an eyebrow in challenge.

He pulls me against him, my breasts flattening against his broad chest. "Don't tell anyone," he growls before kissing me breathless. "Now let's go, before I get an obscene hard-on and can't walk around in public."

With that, he yanks me out of the car and we make our way into the maze of food trucks.

The first one we stop at sells fried PB&J sandwiches, which of course, I have to try. Declan passes on that, but I make him take a bite of mine anyway. Next, we hit up a gyro truck, followed by dumplings, and finally, a dessert truck that sells chocolate-dipped cheesecake on a stick.

Throughout the evening, Declan's hands are on me one way or another, whether we're holding hands, stroking my hair, or pulling me into his side and kissing my temple. Right now, we're walking hand in hand while I eat my cheesecake. Declan, unsurprisingly, passed on dessert, saying he'd get his fill later.

"What are you looking at?" I say before taking another bite of my cheesecake on a stick. His eyes are glued to my lips, which makes me smirk a little bit as I chew. I throw a little moan in there, for good measure.

The soft growl coming from Declan is totally worth it. His eyes are dark as he leans forward. I feel his thumb wipe away some chocolate from the corner of my mouth. I turn my head and suck it off of his finger, making him groan.

"Fuck, Luna..."

I just grin and resume eating my dessert while Declan stares me down. The next thing I know, I'm being pulled into an alleyway, and my cheesecake is tossed to the ground as Declan pushes me up against the brick wall and pins my arms above my head.

"Hey! My cheesecake!" I whine though I'm not really upset with the turn of events.

"I'll buy you the whole damn truck, but I need to kiss you right the fuck now," he all but growls.

Before I can give him some snarky remark, Declan crashes his lips down on mine. I open up for him and he thrusts his tongue into my mouth while grinding his cock into my stomach.

Declan breaks the kiss and releases his grip on me to skim his fingers down my arms before cupping my breasts. His hands roam lower until one is trailing up the inside of my thigh. He rubs his fingers over my pussy, through my tights and panties. I gasp, loving the pressure, but needing more.

Declan proves once again that he knows my body better than I do. His hand slips into my tights and panties, where he teases me with his fingers until finally, one large digit slides through my slit, making me shake with need.

"Jesus, Luna. You're always so wet for me. Love this juicy cunt," he groans.

When he dips two fingers into my entrance, I gasp and lower my hands to his chest, fisting the material of his shirt in my hands. I whimper into the side of his neck while he pumps his large fingers in and out of me and grinds the heel of his hand on my clit.

"Yes, ohmygod..." I say breathlessly, trying to keep my voice down.

"I feel you, Luna. I feel your tight little body trembling for me. Do you need to cum, sweetheart?"

"Yes, God yes..." I moan.

He pinches my clit, sending a jolt of pain and pleasure all over my body.

"How do good girls ask?"

"Please, sir, please make me cum!"

Declan thrusts a third finger deep inside of me, stretching me deliciously wide, and swirls his thumb over my clit while roughly squeezing my breast. I can't help the way my hips grind down on his fingers, trying to get him deeper, deeper, deeper.

"That's it, ride my fucking hand," he grunts

Each swipe of his thumb winds me tighter and tighter. It's all I can focus on; the growing pressure, the intense pleasure bordering on pain, all of it seizing my lungs until I inhale sharply and shatter in his arms. I bite Declan's shoulder to muffle my screams, which makes him grunt and pump his hand faster, sending me up and over again.

I'm a shaky, soggy mess by the time I come down. My hands drop down his chest, his abs, and then I palm his cock. It's the first time I've touched him, and I instantly want more.

"Luna," he groans in warning.

"Please, sir?" I ask.

"Fuck, when you ask so nicely for me..."

I quickly work on undoing his pants and pulling him out. His cock is thick and throbbing in my hand, so big I can hardly wrap my fingers around all of it. I give him a squeeze, loving the way he hisses out a breath.

"Jesus, Luna..."

I feel precum leaking down his shaft, so I wipe it around with my thumb, massaging the head of his cock. More dribbles out, and I rub it up and down, squeezing him and alternating between fast and slow strokes.

He grunts and starts thrusting his fingers in and out of me again, harder and faster than before, making my already swollen pussy tense and flutter around him.

"Fuck, how are you so good at that? I'm about to lose it, sweetheart, I don't want to get your pretty dress all dirty."

"I want you to get all of me dirty," I whisper before sucking on his neck.

"Goddamn," he grunts as he begins swirling his fingers over my clit again.

I gasp for air, panting and shaking in his arms while still stroking his dick. I feel it swell up in my hand, so I pump my hand faster, faster, until I'm about to cramp up, but I keep going, needing him to cum.

I'm so focused on Declan, my own orgasm slams into me almost by surprise. I cry out as my whole body spasms, causing me to fist his cock and squeeze it roughly as I cum long and hard.

"Fuck!" He yells, burying his head into my neck to stifle the sound. I feel hot liquid spurt over my hand, but I keep stroking him, keep feeling him pulse and cum in my hand.

"Fuck," he says again, quieter this time, his voice shaking.

I take my hand away only when I feel him softening. Declan withdraws his fingers from my pussy and rubs my juices on my neck before licking them off. It's fucking hot and has me ready for more of him, even though I just came three times.

When he finally pulls apart from me, I bring my hand, dripping with his release, up to my mouth and lick it off. I wasn't sure what to expect, but his cum tastes salty, spicy, and somehow, just like him. I love it.

"Shit, my dirty little Luna. That was so fucking hot."

I grin at him and he kisses me hard, but quick, growling as he tears his mouth away from mine.

Declan tucks his already half-hard cock back into his pants and helps me straighten my dress. We make our way back to the car, both grinning like fools.

Chapter 13

Luna

I thought for sure Declan and I were going to have sex last night, but when we got back to his place, he led me to the room I stayed in last night and kissed me on the forehead before telling me goodnight. Part of me was disappointed, but another part of me loves that he can read me and that he knew I wasn't quite ready mentally, even if my body sure was.

We're on our way to the hospital now, after a lazy Saturday morning of sleeping in, cooking brunch together, and yeah, some making out, because how could I keep my hands off of someone so ridiculously sexy?

I'm a little apprehensive about Lucas meeting Declan. I told Lucas yesterday about how Declan basically saved me and that we're kind of a thing now. He's skeptical of the whole boss/employee dynamic, though he's grateful I still have a job.

Declan and I stop in front of Lucas' room, where I take a deep breath. Maybe I'm more anxious about this than I thought.

"Are you embarrassed to be seen with an old bastard like me?" He teases.

An unexpected laugh bubbles up from my chest and I shake my head no, peering into those gray eyes of his that are sparkling. I needed a bit of a tension breaker, and Declan seemed to know that too. How does this man already know me better than I know myself?

I walk into the room and tug Declan along, the smile still on my lips.

"About time you got here! Is that boss of yours making you do *special* favors for him on the weekend now?"

"Lucas! Oh my God!" I glare at him and try to force my blush away.

"Hey, Lucas. I'm the boss," Declan says, not missing a beat.

"Hi, bossman. Are you being nice to my sister? Making sure she eats and sleeps? She's not very good at taking care of herself or taking orders."

"Oh, I don't know about that. She takes orders just fine." Declan gets a wicked smile on his face, and I smack him in the chest.

"Declan!"

He laughs, freaking *laughs*, while Lucas mimes gagging and throwing up.

"In a strictly professional setting, of course," Declan says, though his tone indicates that's not at all what he means.

"Uh-huh," Lucas says, though he's hiding a smirk. "If she's happy, I'm happy."

I glare at both of them, and the two of them smile innocently at me. I roll my eyes, but can't help smiling back, even though I'm thoroughly mortified.

We slip into an easy conversation, mostly Declan asking questions and Lucas telling him embarrassing stories about me as a child or pranks we played on each other, but I don't mind. Sitting back and listening to the two of them talk, watching the way Declan is genuinely interested in Lucas while he still keeps a hand on my leg, warms me deep inside. Something clicks into place and I know I'm ready to take things further with him. My body was on board from day one, but my mind needed to catch up. And my heart? It's already his, whether he knows it or not.

Lucas is in the middle of telling Declan about the time I got jealous of his mini-gumball machine and replaced all of the gum with marbles, *billing lady of doom*, comes walking in.

"Luna. Have a few minutes to chat?"

I feel the weight of Lucas' and Declan's stare, both probably wanting me to introduce Karen. Yeah, not happening.

"Sure! You know I love any chance I get to talk to you!" I don't mean for the sarcastic response to slip out, but there it is. I don't even have the excuse of being sleep deprived this time.

Karen narrows her eyes and steps out into the hall, knowing I'll follow.

"Ms. Foster, as I was trying to tell you the other day, we're having some issues with the insurance information you gave us about your current employer, White Knight Advertising. It looks like your policy kicks in after ninety days of employment. But you've only been working there... five weeks, is it?"

The way she asks like it's a question when I know she already knows the answer pisses me off as much as it strikes terror into my very being. *I don't have insurance.* Lucas has had chemo, he's been in the ICU, he's had multiple tests, MRIs, CAT scans, blood tests...

"You don't have to pay everything right now, of course. I know you know that. But we will need to discuss updating your payment plan."

I nod, numbly. "After the insurance kicks in, will it work retroactively?"

By the look on her face, I already know the answer. "I'm sorry, Ms. Foster. That's not how it works. Too bad this couldn't have waited a few months, huh? That's how these things go, so it seems." *Billing lady of doom* laughs, but I don't. It's my fucking life, not a goddamn joke.

She must sense I'm not in the laughing mood, as she sobers up and collects the papers.

"I'll give you some time to... process. We'll be in touch," she says as she heads out of the room.

"I'm sure you will," I grumble.

When the door closes, I drop my head in my hands and allow myself one minute to wallow in self-pity. When my minute is up, I take a breath and put on my cheerleader face. Lucas doesn't need to worry about this.

I walk back to the room have to stifle a laugh when I see Declan and Lucas watching the worst show ever created.

"Seriously? You too?" I ask Declan.

He flashes a smile at me, but then I see it drop ever so slightly, the concern clear in his eyes. How is he so in tune with my feelings?

"Everything okay, hummingbird?"

"*Hummingbird?* Oh my *God*, that's adorable. And nauseating," Lucas jokes.

I roll my eyes at him and shove his feet over so I can sit on the edge of the bed. "You're just jealous that you don't have a cool nickname," I say, ignoring Declan's question altogether. He seems to take the hint and drops the subject.

We finish the episode of *Diners, Drive-Ins, and Dives*, and then Lucas shoos us off when his dinner arrives. I ask him if it's disappointing to eat that crap after watching his favorite show, and he answers by throwing a green bean at me. I smile seeing him like this. Hopefully he can come home soon.

***

Declan cooks us chicken with a mushroom white wine sauce for dinner, and then leads me over to the couch to give me a foot rub once he's built a fire in the huge fireplace.

"Are you going to tell me who that lady was who talked to you at the hospital?"

"Probably not." I give him a playful smile, hoping he'll leave it alone.

"Luna," he says in that tone of his. The one that says he's not backing down.

I sigh and turn my head to the side, suddenly fascinated by the fireplace and looking at it rather than meeting Declan's gaze. "She's from the billing department. Just some details that needed to be worked out."

"You said that earlier when I asked about treatments. What kind of details need to be worked out?"

"Oh, you know. Just sorting through some payments and stuff."

Declan squeezes my foot and tugs a bit, getting me to look at him. "What stuff, Luna?"

I sigh, defeatedly. "I applied for a few programs that supplement certain cancer treatments and medical bills, but I got rejected because I make too much."

He nods, though I can tell he doesn't really get it.

"And today she told me about the insurance..."

His brow furrows, and then understanding spreads across his handsome face. "It doesn't kick in until ninety days."

I nod and shrug. "Yeah, but I just had her add it to my tab. What's a few more bucks in the long run, right?" I try going for nonchalance, but I'm not sure I quite pull it off.

Declan opens his mouth to say something but then shuts it again.

"Look, I don't want to think about it tonight, okay? How hard was Lucas on you while I stepped out?" I plead with him to let me change the subject.

Declan gives me one last knowing look but then answers my question. "He wasn't too harsh. Just gave me the brother talk."

"The brother talk?"

"Hurt her and I'll maim you, break her heart and I'll break your balls, the usual."

"He threatened bodily harm?"

Declan nods solemnly, though his eyes sparkle with playfulness. Good, I want his playful side. His sweet side. His dominant side. Anything that steers us away from the side of him that wants to talk about my money problems.

"It's a good thing I'd never hurt you. I'm quite fond of my appendages. And my balls," he winks at me.

I roll my eyes at him. "Guys and their balls."

He tugs at me again, only this time he grips my calf and pulls me towards him at the same time he's leaning down over me.

"You better not be talking about anyone else's balls, little Luna," he growls, his face hovering mere inches above mine, his body pinning mine to the couch.

"Only yours. *Sir.*"

Declan's eyes flash with a dark hunger, one that tells me he wants me as much as I want him. He drags my bottom lip through his teeth and then plunges his tongue into my mouth, making me moan. His kiss is primal and needy, and I kiss him back, matching every need of his with a need of my own.

"Fuck," he says, breaking our kiss. His hips buck, thrusting his erection up against my core, making me wet and needy.

"I want you, Declan. I want all of you."

He grows still at my words and leans back to look at me.

"Are you sure, sweetheart? Because once we start, I don't know if I'll be able to hold back."

I'm sure that was meant as a warning, but it only makes me hotter for him.

"I'm sure. I ache for you. I feel so empty..."

"Jesus, Luna. When you say shit like that to me it makes me want to rip off all your clothes and tear your little pussy apart."

"Then why don't you?"

His eyes darken and he devours my lips, growling into my mouth and kissing me savagely. Declan breaks our kiss and presses his lips to my forehead, breathing in deep. It's such a contrast to the way he just made my lips numb from his intensity.

"Not this first time, hummingbird," he whispers. "I can't lose control with you."

Declan scoops me up in his arms and carries me to his room. Tossing me on the bed, I bounce twice and then he pounces on me, nuzzling my neck.

Declan rolls on his side, facing me. He reaches out and tucks some hair behind my ear and pulls me in for a soft kiss.

"Are you sure?" He asks me again. "I never want you to regret anything between us, especially our first time together."

"I'm sure," I tell him. I wish there were stronger words, some way to convince him, but everything I can think of just sounds cliché. *I've never felt this way before, I've never wanted anyone the way I want you, I need you...* Instead, I opt for, "I trust you, Declan."

I kiss him this time, pouring out everything I can't seem to say.

The next thing I know, Declan has me on my back and he's looming over me. In this moment, he looks absolutely possessed, like a wild animal. Underneath it though, I still see the way he cares for me. I know he'd never hurt me, which makes me want to unlock the beast I know he's trying to suppress.

I lean up to kiss him again, but he pulls away. I strain my neck higher, but he pulls back farther, grinning as I pout. He gives me a chaste kiss and gets off the bed.

I follow him off of the bed, about to complain, but then I see him take his shirt off, revealing his chest to me for the very first time. Yeah, he's as delicious and sexy and absolutely chiseled as I thought he was. More so, in fact. I can't help but lick my lips as my eyes drift over the unexpected tattoos swirling over one shoulder and down his chest. Then my eyes drop lower to his six-pack, and lower still, to those two sculpted lines leading to his massive dick.

When I finally drag my eyes back up to meet his, he's smirking at me. The cocky bastard.

I start to take my shirt off too, but he reaches out and stops my hands.

"No way, that's my job. Let me unwrap my little Luna. My perfect present."

Declan takes my hands in his, kissing one and then the other, before lifting them above my head. His hands slide down my arms, slowly, burning a path as they go. He cups my breasts and keeps moving his hands down over my ribcage, my tummy, and then he grasps the hem of my shirt and lifts it up over my head in one fluid motion.

My bra comes off next, and then he's kneeling down in front of me, kissing a trail down my tummy. He bites the waistband of my pants and tugs, chuckling when I gasp. Declan works the button with his deft fingers and slowly peels my pants off along with my panties, helping me step out of them one leg at a time.

I feel his hands skim up the back of my calves, my thighs, my ass, and then he pulls me forward so he can kiss my pussy. My inner muscles clench with desire, and I know he sees my juices dripping down the inside of my thighs.

"Goddamn," he groans before leaning down and licking up my arousal. Declan dips his tongue inside of my slit and then pushes me back on the bed, making me squeal.

He spreads my thighs apart and guides one leg over his shoulder, and then the other, opening me up for him. Then, Declan dives into my soaking wet cunt, making me cry out with the feeling of his hot mouth on my most private place.

He begins slowly, with long waves of his tongue that roll up and down inside my pussy. Just when I need more, his thumb finds my clit and rubs circles around the little ball of nerves while he continues to lick me and suck on my folds.

An index finger slides inside of me with ease, then a middle finger joins as he pistons in and out of me with his muscular arm, fucking me into the bed. He rotates his fingers and pauses to look up at me, grinning with mischief. Then he curls his fingers up and finds that secret spot, rubbing his fingers against it and watching me tense and moan as he completely destroys me with his fingers.

"Yes, oh yes," I cry out, unable to stop myself.

He growls into my pussy, making my clit vibrate with his voice. Declan slides and twists and rubs the walls of my pussy with his fingers while his tongue does wicked things to my little bundle of nerves. He licks it, bats it around, and finally sucks it into his mouth and bites down gently, causing my orgasm to rip through me and spill all over his fingers.

I buck my hips as he sticks his tongue in my entrance, lapping up everything I'm giving him.

When I finally come back down to earth, I sink into the mattress. Declan climbs on top of me, propping himself up on one elbow while his other hand cups my face. He presses gentle kisses all over with featherlight touches of his lips. He tickles my forehead, nose, cheeks, and finally, my mouth. Declan strokes his tongue inside of me slowly, deliberately, while his hand moves from my face and trails down my body, caressing me and setting me on fire.

I spread my legs and welcome more of his skin on my skin. At some point, Declan rid himself of his pants and boxers. I feel his hot, hard cock rubbing against my pussy.

In a sudden surge of confidence, I push against Declan's chest, urging him to sit up.

"Everything okay, hummingbird?"

"I want to see you," I breathe out, my heart hammering in my chest.

Declan grins and stands up. I sit on the edge of the bed and take him in for the first time. All of him. Even though I just saw his chest moments ago, I'm still surprised at how muscled and perfect he is. And then there's his thick, glorious cock that I know is going to stretch me and break me in the most exquisite way. I stand up and place my hands on his bare chest, loving the feeling of his warm skin and how his muscles tense and flex underneath my fingers.

Declan throws his head back and hisses out a breath. "God, your touch, Luna... It undoes me."

I smile and continue my exploration, trailing my hands over the dips and curves of his sculpted body, followed by my tongue. I can't explain it, but I want to taste him, his sweat, his skin, and yeah, I want to taste his cum again. Only this time I want it straight from the source.

I start to kneel before him, but Declan grabs my arms and pulls me up into a kiss.

"The first time I cum tonight is going to be in your tight little pussy, Luna, not your mouth."

"The first time?" I ask, half-joking, half nervous for what all that implies.

"Mmhmm," he says, nuzzling my neck and kissing me there. "I'm going to make you cum on my cock a few times before I empty myself deep inside of you. Then I'll lap up our mess and have you ride my face until you cum again. When you think you can't take anymore, I'll sink inside of you and make us cum together again and again until the only thing you remember is how my fat cock feels as it's ripping you apart."

"Oh fuck," I moan as he nips at my ear and licks my pulse point. "Please do that to me. Please, sir."

"Jesus," he groans, pushing me back on the bed and climbing on top of me again.

Declan holds himself up with a forearm on either side of my head. I spread my legs once again, welcoming all of him. I feel him rub his dick through my folds, moaning when he hits my clit. I wrap my legs around his hips and try to pull him where I need him most. All of this teasing and dirty talk has me desperate to finally have him inside of me.

My movement has the opposite effect that I want. Instead of entering me, Declan pulls back and kisses away my protests.

"Let me do this, Luna. Give me control," he whispers into my lips before kissing me sweetly, passionately.

When we pull apart, I feel his right hand slipping in between our bodies as he fists his cock and guides it to my entrance.

"Are you ready, hummingbird?"

"Yes, sir," I whimper, the excitement and anxiety swirling in my stomach.

Declan pushes inside of me, slowly, watching my reaction. I feel myself stretching, almost to the point of pain. It burns a little bit, but I still want more. Declan is shaking as he tries to restrain himself. He continues his slow invasion of me until I feel him bump up against my barrier.

I gasp and close my eyes, preparing for him to enter me completely.

"Look at me, Luna. I want to watch you as I claim you for the first time."

My eyes snap open, and Declan pulls back slightly so he can rub my clit with his thumb. It relaxes me a little bit.

"Mine," he growls as he thrusts all the way inside of me, hitting home. I feel a pinch deep in my core, and a pain that ripples out of me, making me cry out.

Declan doesn't move, he just stays still as I adjust to this new feeling.

"Breathe for me, baby," he whispers before kissing my forehead. "I'm sorry I had to hurt you. It gets better, sweet Luna. I promise I'll make you feel so good."

I take a deep breath and stare into those beautiful eyes of his. They are full of such emotion, such warmth, and concern. I truly feel like I'm the most important thing in the world to him right now.

"I'm okay," I tell him. "I trust you, sir."

"Love when you call me that. But I love that you trust me even more. How are you feeling, sweetheart?"

"So full...but good. It doesn't hurt much anymore."

"Can I move?" He grits out, the restraint slipping from him each second he's not moving inside of me.

I nod my approval.

"Need you to tell me what you want, Luna."

"I want you to move. Fuck me, sir."

"Fuck," he grunts, pulling out and thrusting into me again.

We both groan when he hits home over and over. I love feeling the thick veins in his cock sliding against the walls of my pussy as he moves in and out of me.

"So goddamn tight, Jesus, you feel so good, little Luna."

"You...too..." I manage to say in between thrusts. I wrap my arms around his back and grip the taut muscles there, clinging to him while he picks up speed.

Declan twists his hips slightly, changing up the angle. He hits that spot inside of me with his dick, making my whole body jerk in his arms.

"Does that feel good?" He asks.

"Y-yes..." I moan.

I dig my nails into his back to spur him on. Declan crashes his mouth down on mine as our bodies come together, again and again, flesh meeting flesh, pleasure meeting pleasure. I squeeze my legs around him and clench my pussy to get him deeper inside of me.

Declan thrusts into me harder, faster, each stroke of his dick pushing me closer, closer, hitting that spot over and over, once, twice, again, again, *fuck*, one more time, please, please, I need it, my body trembling and aching for more.

He slams into me one last time and I scream, shattering around him. My pussy clamps down on his thick cock as all my muscles tense up tightly and then unwind, the orgasm rolling through me in explosive waves.

"That's it, sweetheart, that's so fucking it, cum for me again, Luna."

I shake my head, unable to imagine myself doing that again. Declan, however, doesn't take no for an answer. He leans back and sits on his heels, grabbing my hips and fucking himself with my body. The angle is different, deeper, hitting new places that make me shake and moan uncontrollably.

"Oh, God, Declan. This is..."

I gasp and cry out as I feel his fingers blurring over my clit. With one pinch, he has me twisting in his arms, but he won't let me escape the onslaught of sensations as my orgasm claws at me and rips me apart from the inside out. I thrash and scream as Declan continues to fuck me through it.

"Look at us, Luna," he demands, his voice gravelly and desperate. "Look how your pussy stretches and takes my big cock like a good girl. You're fucking incredible. Fuck!"

I open my eyes as my orgasm fades and see him sink into me again and again. It's fucking dirty and hot as hell. His movements become jerky and I feel his dick swell up, growing impossibly larger. He's throbbing and thrusting and working me up into another orgasm, both of us sweating and shaking.

Then he pulls himself out and strokes himself once before spraying his cum all over my tits and stomach.

"Fuck, fuck, fuck, Luna," he groans. "Mine, fucking *mine*."

The next second, Declan is kneeling in between my legs, licking my swollen pussy as he rubs his cum into my skin. The feeling of his hot seed cooling against my skin, his tongue dipping into my entrance, his teeth scraping against my clit, has me bowing my back of the bed and climaxing so hard I can't breathe.

Barely giving me any time to recover, Declan flips me on my stomach and plunges his already hard cock inside of me. Cum coats my thighs as my cunt snaps around his huge dick. He pounds into me mercilessly, making obscene noises as he fucks me into yet another blinding orgasm, sobbing my release. This time, I take him with me over the edge. I feel him shoot his load deep inside of me, rope after rope until he is spent.

I must have passed out there for a second because when I open my eyes, Declan has me wrapped up in his arms and he's pressing soft kisses over my face and neck.

"Are you okay?" He sounds panicked, almost.

"What?" I ask in total confusion. "Declan, that...I don't even know how to describe it. I didn't know I could feel so incredible."

His hands come up to cradle my face as he searches my eyes for truth. When he's satisfied with what he sees, Declan closes his eyes and rests his forehead on mine, breathing in deeply.

"Luna. My little Luna," he whispers more to himself than to me. "Fuck, you're perfect, you know that? So perfect."

Declan strokes my hair and continues whispering sweet things to me until my breathing evens out and my heart rate slows.

"Come on, hummingbird. Let me wash you up."

Declan starts to untangle himself from me, but I tighten my hold on him. He chuckles and kisses my forehead.

"I made you all dirty, sweetheart. You gotta let me clean you so I can make you all filthy again."

I grin at him and let him get up. Declan bends down and scoops me up in his arms, kissing me the whole way to the bathroom where he runs a bath for us. He sets me down in the water so gently before climbing in behind me and washing every part of me with such care.

We dry off and he carries me to bed where he tells me I'm beautiful and perfect and sweet and his. The last thing I remember is him turning me on my side so he can spoon around me and kiss me on my neck. I swear he said he's never letting me go.

Chapter 14

Luna stirs in my arms and lets out a little contented sigh. It's just after seven-thirty in the morning, but I've been up for hours just watching her sleep. Obsessive, I know, but I'm way past caring at this point.

She's so fucking beautiful. I was already so far gone for her before last night, but after being inside of her, feeling her cum around me, seeing her absolutely break apart for me again and again...well, shit, I don't think I can ever let her go. I told her that last night as we were falling asleep, but I don't know if she heard me.

Has it really only been two days since I picked her up at that shitty bus stop? How has she woven herself into the very fabric of my being so quickly? If I'm honest with myself, I think it started the first time I laid eyes on her. She's held me captive ever since.

Every new thing I learn about Luna only fuels my obsession with her. After we had lunch together all those weeks ago, I thought she was too sweet, too naïve for someone like me. And while she is sweet and far too good for me, she's also resilient. Brave. Fierce. She's been touched by tragedy, but instead of caving under pressure, she stood up to the challenge and fought for a better life for her and Lucas.

Luna mumbles something in her sleep, which makes me smile. It's still a new thing for me, this whole smiling business. I can't say I don't like it. At least around her. My dad always said vulnerability is a weakness, but around Luna, I feel strong. She makes me want to take on the whole fucking world for her. I'd give her anything if only she'd ask.

But I know she won't. Which is why I plan on spoiling her every second of every day. Starting right now.

I slide the covers off of us and kiss my way down Luna's incredible body. I settle in between her legs and part them, looking at her perfect little pussy. I suppress a groan when I see she's already wet for me. My dirty little Luna. I flatten my tongue and drag it up her delicious cunt, sucking on her clit when I get to the top.

Luna moans softly, though I can tell she's still sleeping. I continue sucking on her folds, licking up every inch of her sweet pussy, and finally, I spear my tongue in her entrance.

This gets her attention.

"Declan? Oh fuck, ohmygod," she gasps.

I feel her hands on my head, tugging at my hair and pushing me closer. I chuckle at her eagerness, which makes her moan again. I'm suffocating on her intoxicating pussy, and there's nowhere else I'd rather be.

When I have to lift my head up for air, I see Luna's beautiful olive eyes staring down at me in awe and lust. It's one of my favorite looks of hers, and I vow to make her look at me like that every morning for the rest of our lives. Yeah, I'm *that* far gone for her, and she has no idea.

I place one hand in between her perfect little breasts and slide it down her body. She arches her back at my touch, which thrusts her wet, hot cunt into my face. Taking the hint, I get back to work, alternating fast and slow strokes, hard and soft strokes, until Luna is whimpering and writhing at the tip of my tongue.

"I need to cum, sir. I need to cum so fucking bad," she cries out, bucking her hips and riding my face.

I growl and bite down on her clit, causing her to convulse and soak my face with her release. I drink down her essence and place sloppy kisses up her body until I take her mouth. Luna kisses me right back and then licks her cream off of my chin.

"Jesus, dirty girl. You like how you taste?"

"Mmhmm..." she says all breathy and sexy as fuck before she bites my lip and kisses me again.

When we break apart, I see her eyes glossed over, her pupils blown wide with lust. She gets a wicked grin on her face that makes my cock twitch. Luna buries her face in my neck and nips my skin, causing me to groan.

"Your turn," she whispers before shoving me off of her with a surprising force.

Before I can even register her words, Luna straddles me and kisses the fuck out of me. She gets me all worked up and then rips her mouth away from mine, making me growl in frustration. Luna just smiles and then kisses her way down my chest, scooting down my body, kissing my abs, lower, lower, till she's between my legs, kissing the tip of my swollen cock.

"Holy fuck," I hiss, gritting my teeth together.

"Teach me?" She asks with equal parts innocence and sincerity.

"Baby, there's no way to do this wrong. Do what comes naturally, it'll be amazing because you're amazing."

She hesitates for a second, biting her bottom lip. Goddamn, the way she's staring at my dick has me leaking precum. This must snap her out of her insecurities, because next thing I know, she's licking up the little liquid pearl and then putting her mouth around me.

"Jesus, woman," I grunt. She's hardly even done anything yet and I'm already on edge. I fist the sheets, resisting the urge to grab her head and fuck her mouth. It's too soon for that.

Luna smiles with my dick in her mouth, which is ridiculously sweet and sexy and perfectly Luna. She bobs her head up and down, taking in a little more of me each time. Then she fucking shoves her face down on me until I hit the back of her throat. She gags around my cock and my hand finds the back of her head. It takes every single ounce of control I have not to shove her down even more so she's deep throating me. Instead, I weave my fingers in her hair and tug her back a bit.

"Relax, sweetheart. You're so beautiful giving me pleasure like this. Breathe, baby."

She breathes through her nose and starts sucking on me again, massaging the underside of my cock with her tongue.

"That's it, Luna, fuck, that's so fucking it," I groan.

She scrapes her nails over my balls, making me tighten my grip on her hair and buck my hips. I worry that I was too rough, but then she fucking moans and takes me deeper.

"So good, baby, so fucking good."

Luna is perfect, already a pro at reading my body and responding. She cups my balls and sucks me into the back of her throat again, swallowing around the head of my cock.

"I'm close, shit, sweetheart..."

Fuck, I want to cum down her throat so badly, but I want to be inside of her little cunt more. I pull on her hair, popping her off of my dick. She pouts, which makes me chuckle.

"Need inside that little pussy of yours," I say by way of explanation. She licks her lips and nods as she climbs up my body and straddles me. "You want to ride me, dirty girl?"

She nods and bites her lip, so damn sexy and eager.

I slide my hands up her legs and grip her hips, holding her above my aching cock.

"Ask me nicely," I growl.

"Please, sir, let me ride your big fat cock."

"Fucking Christ, Luna, that mouth of yours. Shit. Use me, baby girl, use me for your pleasure."

Luna nods and then drops herself down on me in one swift motion, making us both cry out.

"Take it slow, sweetheart, you have to be sore from last night."

"I'm okay, I just want you so much. Is that bad? I feel like I'm going crazy."

I reach out and tuck some hair behind her ear, sliding my hand around to the back of her neck so I can pull her down for a kiss.

"It's not bad, hummingbird. Fuck, I want you too, so much. I'm glad I'm not the only one going crazy."

I slide my hands down her back and grip her ass, helping her grind down on me until she finds what feels good. Luna braces herself with a hand on either side of my head, placing her delicious tits right in my face. I suck on her breasts and bite her nipples while Luna rolls her hips and fucks me with everything she has.

"Declan! Oh fuck..."

Luna tenses and buries her head in my neck as her entire body goes still. Then, all at once, she loses control, her body spasming around me. She bites my neck, and fucking gushes all over me, her release dripping down my balls.

I grab her ass, pulling her cheeks apart, and fuck up into her, grunting each time I hit home. Luna cries out and a fresh wave of wetness coats me as she cums again, her pussy choking the life out of my dick.

With a roar, I shoot my load deep inside of her, filling her so full it leaks out of her pussy. The bed is a fucking mess, sloppy with our combined orgasms, which only makes everything that much hotter.

Luna takes a shuddering breath and then goes limp in my arms, her little heart beating so fast in her chest. I wrap my arms around her and hold her close as we both come back to earth.

We don't say anything for a while. I stroke her back with one hand while the other grips her ass possessively, holding her close to me.

"Is it always going to be that good?" Luna whispers, making me smile. She's fucking adorable and incredible and mine. I can't believe I found her and that she's somehow deemed me worthy of her presence.

"Yeah, little hummingbird. It'll always be good because it's you and me."

She pops her little head up and smiles at me. I'm fucking blown away by her beauty every single time.

"You and me," she confirms, kissing me to seal in the declaration.

***

After showering together and getting breakfast, Luna and I head over to the hospital to see Lucas. After chatting and turning on the tv, I slip out of Lucas' room, saying I need to go to the restroom. Once outside, I follow the signs to the billing office, knowing I'm about to do something Luna needs, but will ultimately hate.

"Can I help you?"

"Yes, I'm here to pay off the remainder of an account."

The lady behind the desk looks at me like I grew a second head. I'm sure she doesn't get many people in here who are able to pay off the entirety of a cancer patient's bill in one sitting.

"Uh, yes, well, of course, let me help you with that. Who is the patient?"

"Lucas Foster."

"Okay, let me pull up his account... Oh. Are you sure you want to pay the remaining balance? It's quite extensive. And it looks like the payments are a few months late."

"I'm positive."

"Mister...?"

"Knight. Declan Knight."

"Mr. Knight. It will be one hundred and eighty thousand dollars to clear the slate, so to speak, but Lucas is currently still in the hospital, and he will likely need more treatments."

The amount shocks me, not because I can't afford it – in fact, that kind of money is nothing to me. With or without the company, my brothers and I are billionaires thanks to the inheritance and some well-timed investments. No, I'm shocked that Luna has had to carry this burden for so long. I'm sure it feels totally insurmountable to be drowning in debt like this.

I know Luna will be pissed if getting her car out of the impound lot is any indication, but she'll have to understand that I only want the best for her and Lucas, right?

"Mr. Knight?" The lady's voice cuts through my thoughts.

"Yes, that's fine. Put it all on here," I say matter-of-factly, handing her my black AmEx card. Her overly-plucked eyebrows disappear into her hairline as she stares at the card. "And please keep that card on file for future charges."

Once the interaction is over, I make my way back to Lucas and Luna. I hope she can see my good intentions, especially after everything we shared last night and this morning.

Chapter 15

Luna

Declan dropped me off at my apartment last night after spending all weekend together. It's amazing to think about how much we've shared in such a short time. Not just the sex and all of the orgasms, though those were amazing and life-altering, it was how he held me after, the way he took care of me and knew just what to say.

But now it's Monday morning and I'm not sure where we stand. Declan isn't much of a texter, and therefore we haven't spoken since we parted ways last night.

I told myself it was fine, and I shouldn't read into it. That lasted all of twenty minutes. By three in the morning, I had convinced myself that Declan is going to fire me and then we'll be homeless and I'll have to sneak Lucas off to Mexico so we can get treatment for his cancer from some doctor who works for the cartel and runs a side business helping people in need as a way to offset his conscience about his involvement in a gang.

I went to sleep with that last scene running through my head and then dreamed about Declan coming to find us and saving the day. The dream turned rather dirty after that, so I woke up this morning not only confused and anxious but horny as hell.

Happy Monday to me.

I've been in the office for about an hour now, sipping coffee and catching up on meeting notes and emails I missed while I've been away. I came in early so I could try and get caught up before Declan gets here. Even the thought of seeing him again has me blushing.

"You're...here?" A shrill voice says from behind me. I turn to see Tiffany with her hands on her hips, eyeing me with disbelief.

"Yup. Just catching up on emails," I say in my most professional *I'm busy please fuck off* tone.

"But you...you just left. And now..."

"I'm back."

"Declan's going to fire you, you know. You can't just *walk out* and then come back in and have a job. He's going to fire you for sure. Does he know you're back?" She looks at me incredulously.

Just then, Declan steps out of the elevator. He's as handsome as always with his black, wavy hair styled just so, his piercing gray eyes, his sharp, angled jaw, now rid of the stubble he'd been rocking the last few days with me. God, the insides of my thighs burn at the memory of him licking my pussy and scraping his stubbled chin against the soft skin there.

"Luna," Declan says by way of greeting. His tone is cold and detached. He doesn't even look at me before he turns and goes into his office, slamming his door.

Well, shit.

The day moves slowly as I work through projects, organize notes, and schedule everything. Every time I get an email or a notification on my phone, I think it's going to be Declan firing me or Declan saying something sweet, but it never is. He hasn't acknowledged me at all.

Not even when he left for lunch.

Three hours ago.

Now it's three-thirty and I'm a ball of nerves. Did this last weekend mean nothing to him? Maybe he's not going to fire me, but it appears things are going right back to the way they were before I left. I don't know which is worse. How can I go back to seeing Declan as my cold, distant boss after knowing he can be sweet and tender? How can I be around him every day but actually *be* with him? What was this whole weekend even about? Am I being the cliché virgin who is clinging to the guy and reading far too much into his every word? How will I...

"Luna," Declan barks as he storms in from the elevator. "My office. Five minutes."

I nod and try to take a deep breath. I guess this is it. He's going to fire me after all.

Tiffany makes a disapproving "tsk-tsk" sound.

"I can start boxing up your...*things*," she says as she gives the stink eye to all of my decorations.

"Don't you dare touch my stuff," I snap at her.

Tiffany walks around to the front of my desk, blocking my view of Declan's office.

"Listen here, *Luna*. You're not special. Even if he doesn't fire you—"

"Tiffany," Declan all but growls behind her. "Go get me coffee."

"But—"

"From Café Giorgio."

"Mr. Knight—"

"Now!" Declan barks.

Tiffany scrambles away from my desk so fast she almost trips on her four inch heels. I'd laugh, but I'm trying not to throw up from nerves. Declan simply stands by my desk and waits for me to walk ahead of him into his office.

I step inside and the hear Declan come in behind me, closing the door with a click. The next thing I know, I'm pressed against the door with Declan's tongue in my mouth. One large hand pins my wrists above my head while his other hand squeezes my ass and presses me closer to him.

"Goddamnit, Luna, I can't concentrate on anything with you just a few feet away from me," he groans, trailing bites and kisses down my neck. "All I can think about is how your skin feels against mine, how sweet your pussy tastes, what it feels like when you cum on my cock. Fuck, little Luna, you've completely ruined me for anyone else." Declan releases my wrists and surprises me by kissing my forehead.

"So you're not going to fire me?" I whisper.

I feel him smile against my forehead, and then a chuckle rumbles out of his chest. The vibration rolls through me everywhere we're connected.

He finally leans back so he can look me in the eyes. "No, little hummingbird. I said you could work here as long as you want to. Do you still want to?"

"Yes, please...sir," I bite my lip and smile up at him. Now that I'm not worried about losing Declan and my job, all of the anxiety gives way to need.

"Fuuuuck," he groans. "What else do you want?" He asks, kissing me on the lips. "I'll give you anything. Everything."

"You. I want you."

Declan growls and kisses down my neck, unbuttoning the first two buttons of my purple blouse.

"Be more specific, little Luna. What do you want from me? What can I give you, right here, right now?"

He undoes more buttons and kisses in between my breasts before palming one in each hand.

I moan softly when his thumbs caress my hard nipples through the sheer fabric of my bra.

"I want to cum," I whimper.

Declan pinches both of my nipples, sending a jolt of pain throughout my body, followed quickly by heat and pleasure. I gasp and then moan, my body and mind not even sure how to process the duel sensations.

"Ask me nicely," Declan growls, his gray eyes turning charcoal.

"Please make me cum, sir."

Declan kisses me roughly and then tears his mouth away. He backs up, leaving me slumped against the wall. He locks the door and closes the blinds so we're in complete privacy in his office. The thought makes my pulse race and my pussy throb.

I watch as he removes his suit jacket and rolls up the sleeves of his white button-down shirt. God, even just watching his forearms flex makes me ache with need. I can't believe this man is mine, that he wants to be with me, that he's *distracted* by me.

He removes his tie and then gives me a wicked grin as he steps closer to where I am.

"Do you trust me, Luna?"

"Yes," I whisper.

He quirks an eyebrow up, his body so close to mine but not touching. I can feel heat and arousal rippling off him, the anticipation of what's to come zipping around us. He's still staring at me, waiting for something. And then I realize my mistake.

"Yes, sir. I trust you."

"Good girl," he praises, giving me a quick, chaste kiss. Declan peels my already unbuttoned blouse off and kisses my right shoulder. "Turn around and cross your wrists behind your back."

I do as he says, gasping when he starts to wrap his silk tie around my wrists. The thought of being tied up in my boss's office should scare me or at the very least, make me ashamed of some of my life choices.

But I'm not scared or ashamed. I'm incredibly turned on. My pussy clenches as Declan ties the final knot and guides me until I'm standing in front of his desk. He skims his hands over my stomach and breasts as he kisses the back of my neck and nips my shoulders.

"So damn beautiful, hummingbird," he whispers in my ear. "Now bend over for me."

Declan places a hand between my shoulder blades, bending me over his desk with my cheek pressed against the cool surface. I gasp when Declan kicks my feet apart so my legs are spread.

"Fucking Christ," Declan growls. "Do you know how many times I've pictured you just like this? How many times I wanted to call you in here and strip you down so I could tongue your pussy and finally have a taste of your sweetness?"

He trails the tips of his fingers down my spine and then swats my ass, making me gasp.

"Answer me. Do you know how many times I've wanted to bend you over my desk and fuck you?"

"N-No…"

He spanks me this time, the sound echoing in the room. The sting comes and goes, leaving a burning desire in its wake. I feel myself growing shamefully wet.

"No, who?"

"No, sir," I moan.

"Mmm, that's my good girl," he says, rubbing my ass where he spanked me. "I've wanted you like this for too damn long. And we're going to make up for lost time."

He kneels behind me, sliding his arms up my legs and pushing my skirt up over my hips, revealing my lacy pink underwear that does nothing to hide my arousal.

"Jesus, Luna. You're so fucking wet. You like being tied up in your boss' office?"

I whimper in response, unable to find my voice just yet.

"You like when I spank you and make your pussy drip? Right here in the middle of the workday?"

"Mmhm…"

He spanks my ass again and then grips my cheek in his hand.

"Yes!" I say a little too loudly.

Declan chuckles. "You have to be quiet for me, dirty girl. Can you do that?"

"Yes, sir," I say quietly.

I feel Declan nuzzle his nose against my pussy, over the now ruined fabric of my panties. His hands massage circles into my legs as they work from my calves up to my thighs. Then, Declan hooks his thumbs into the waistband of my panties and slides them down my legs helping me step out of them.

At this angle, I feel so exposed, both physically and emotionally. Heat spreads through me with the knowledge of how wrong this all is, and yet I feel right. I still feel safe. On edge, yes, pushing my boundaries, definitely, but still so safe.

All my thoughts fly right out of my head when I feel Declan pressing his tongue into my soaking wet folds.

"Oh god," I whisper, biting my lip to keep from crying out.

Declan doesn't start nice and slow. There's no build-up. He's eating me out in sloppy strokes of his tongue that make my pussy gush and flutter. He growls into my cunt, making my legs shake. Declan grips my thighs in his large, strong hands to keep me steady.

I feel his tongue slowly drag from my clit down to my entrance, where he scoops out my juices and brings them back, back, back, until...

Oh my God...

His tongue swirls the puckered flesh of my asshole, making me gasp.

"I'm going to love breaking you in, baby girl. This ass is mine, do you understand?"

"Yes, sir," I squeak out.

He grunts in approval and then spreads my cheeks wide, licking around my little rosebud and sucking, creating an intense pressure that floods my pussy. Declan alternates between eating out my ass and cunt, driving me closer, closer, closer, and then switching, just to start the process over again.

"Declan, sir, please, please..." I beg. My bones are liquid, my muscles sore and tired from straining, again and again, getting right to the edge of release only to be pulled back again.

He sucks on my clit and swirls his tongue around the bundle of nerves once, twice, God one more...one more...

Declan pulls away and stands up, making me growl in frustration. I hear his zipper and then a second later, Declan slams into me, his fat cock pushing me right over the edge into a mind-numbing orgasm. His hand covers my mouth right before I cry out, his other hand wrapping around my hips to hold me in place while he fucks me hard and fast.

"Jesus, Luna..."

He grunts and thrusts into me again and again as papers fall off his desk. The computer monitor rattles and a mug of pens falls to the floor. His hand moves from my mouth to my hair, fisting it and yanking my head back while he picks up his speed.

Declan pistons in and out of me, making wet smacking sounds with each stroke of his cock. He spanks me once, twice, three times, and then grabs my ass and spreads me open wide for him.

"Love watching this juicy cunt swallow my dick, baby girl. You're so fucking perfect, Luna, goddamn."

His fist tightens around my hair, pulling the strands tight against my scalp and electrocuting my nerves. Declan's other hand strokes my clit. I whimper with each thrust of his hips, that thick cock hitting me so, so deep.

"Are you going to cum for me, dirty girl? Are you going to cum all over your boss' desk?"

"Yes, yes, sir, please make me cum..."

Declan growls and pinches my clit, making me convulse in his arms as my orgasm sweeps through me and drains all the air from my lungs.

He continues to piston in and out of me, leaning down and covering my back with his front. Declan swells inside of me and bites my shoulder as he cums in overwhelming waves. I feel his warm release drip down my thighs, making me shudder at the filthiness of it all.

Once his orgasm has faded, Declan unties my wrists and turns me around, helping me sit on his desk. He grabs some tissues from and cleans me up before wrapping his arms around me and holding me close to his chest.

"That was incredible, Luna," he says, kissing the top of my head. "Are you okay? Was that too much?"

"It was so...hot," I whisper, my cheeks burning with equal parts embarrassment and arousal.

Declan chuckles and kisses me so sweetly, nibbling on the bottom lip before pulling away. "Yeah, it was, sweetheart."

I open my mouth to ask him if we can schedule a similar meeting every afternoon this week, but Declan takes a step back and tucks his still half-hard cock away before handing me my blouse.

"I sent Tiffany to a coffee shop twenty minutes away, but she will probably be back soon," he says, putting his jacket and tie back on.

"Sneaky, Mr. Knight. Is that what you had her do with your other assistants, too?" I meant it as a joke, but as soon as I spoke the words out loud, I wanted to take them back.

"Look at me, hummingbird," Declan commands, cupping my chin in his hand. "I've never done an office romance before. Hell, I've hardly done *any* romance before. There hasn't been anyone else in here like this, Luna. Just you." He kisses me so sweetly, wiping away my doubts with every stroke of his tongue. "Only you," he whispers before kissing my forehead.

I smile at him and straighten out my clothes and hair.

"Oh! Where are my panties?"

"Somewhere safe," Declan says, his voice low and gravelly.

My mouth hangs open as he just smiles and winks at me.

"Of all the inappropriate, sexy, dirty things we've done today, *that* is the one that shocked you?" He teases.

"Oh, I've been plenty shocked today, *sir*. You just didn't get to see my face because you had me tied up and bent over your desk. Maybe next time I can tie you up?"

Declan growls and opens his mouth to say something, but I unlock his door and sashay over to my desk, throwing him what I hope is a flirty look over my shoulder. He grins and shakes his head, which makes my tummy erupt in butterflies.

A minute later, the elevator dings and Tiffany stumbles out with a coffee in her hand, looking thoroughly pissed off. Her eyes bug out of her head when she sees me sitting at my desk typing away at my keyboard.

I can't help the smug smile that spreads over my face as I dutifully ignore her and type out an email. I have a feeling Declan is going to give me a lot of reasons to smile in the future.

***

I could smash Declan's stupid, handsome, jerk face right now. I haven't stopped clenching my teeth and scowling since I stormed out of the hospital after my visit with Lucas today.

The doctor told me Lucas would be discharged in the morning, which meant I had to go talk to billing lady of doom to work out my new payment plan. Only, I don't have anything left to pay. Not only that, but all future procedures and treatments are taken care of as well.

I'm so livid right now, like actually burning with anger. I had to pull over *twice* on my way to Declan's because my hands were shaking so bad.

So now I'm parked in the guest spot in the underground lot of his building, trying to calm the fuck down. I need to be able to form actual thoughts and words when I throw them at Declan, which means I need to rein it in a bit.

I slam the door of my car and practically punch the button for his penthouse suite. We made plans for a quiet dinner tonight, but it looks things won't be so quiet after all. I've got a few choice words, all of which will be screamed until he understands what a colossal mistake he just made.

I feel like a caged animal, a bull in a pen, so to speak, just waiting for those elevator doors to open up so I can tell Declan I don't need anything from anyone.

Instead, to my absolute horror, when the doors open and I see Declan standing there waiting for me, I start crying.

Which makes me even angrier.

Declan's face falls and he rushes towards me, but I bat his hands away, so I can step around him.

"Luna, what's—"

"Take it back!" I sob. "I don't want your money, I'm not...I'm not your *whore*!"

Declan recoils as if I hit him, and I don't blame him. Where did that thought even come from? I didn't realize that's how I felt until it just came tumbling out of my mouth.

He closes the distance between us and wraps me up in his arms. I try shoving him off, but I'm no match for his six-foot-three frame and thick muscles.

"Stop! Let me go!" I cry, stupid tears clogging my throat as I continue to ineffectively pound my fists on his chest.

"Baby, please, let me explain," he says in a calming voice.

"It's self-explanatory. We had sex and then you paid me a hundred and eighty thousand dollars." Hearing the words out loud send another punch to my gut, this time the realization knocks all of the air from my lungs.

"Luna, love, please take a breath. Just breathe for me, sweetheart, you're going to hyperventilate."

"Fuck you," I choke out, but it's weak and my voice shakes like the rest of me.

Declan just holds me and strokes my back while looking me over with such concern, coaxing me to breathe with him. He scoops me up in his arms and walks through his apartment until we reach the couch in front of the fireplace, where he has a large fire going.

When he sits down with me in his lap, I instinctively curl up into his chest, my mind and body at war once again. This time, my body wants to seek solace in his strength, while my mind wants to go toe to toe and tell him to back the fuck off.

Declan squeezes me tightly and kisses the top of my head before nudging me up so I have to look at him.

"You are not a whore, Luna. You are so precious to me. It hurts so fucking bad that you think I would treat you that way, that I would treat anyone that way. Do you really think that?"

"Yes. No...I don't know. No, I don't really think that about you, I just...I'm so angry. Why would you do this when you know I can't pay you back?"

"I care about you. And about Lucas. We're together now, hummingbird, I thought you and I already established that."

I nod, trying to reel in the crazy.

"What we've shared is so much more than sex, Luna. You have to know that. It's more than physical for me, it always has been."

I shrug and look away from him, but Declan cups my chin and brings my face back towards his.

"I don't know what sex is normally like, what feelings are supposed to be involved. I didn't know if I was just romanticizing everything..."

He kisses my forehead and then rests his there. "All I know is that I've never felt anything like this, hummingbird. You consume me. I meant what I said today in my office. You've completely ruined me for anyone else. Before you..." he sighs and leans back like he's trying to gather his thoughts. "Before you, I truly thought some part of me was missing. Defective. Broken. But I liked it that way. It made me successful and cutthroat, which were two traits my dad admired. Then one day you came bursting into my life with your pink and teal and glitter and I've never been the same."

I'm trying to smile at him, but those tears are back in full force now. At least this time they are happy tears. His confession soothes my anger, though there are still some lingering fears. Declan wipes away my tears and gives me a sweet kiss on the lips.

"Tell me what you're thinking, little Luna."

"I'm afraid to need you," I whisper. "I'm afraid you'll get so wound up in my heart and in my life that I'll shatter completely when you leave."

"I'm not leaving. I promise," he says, cupping the side of my neck and rubbing his thumb across my jawline.

"You say that now, but what if you walk out like my dad did? Or what if you die like my mom? What if you get sick? I'll be all alone because I'm always alone! I have Lucas, but who knows for how long? And even on the good days...it's so fucking hard doing all of it, Declan, so exhausting all the time and I feel like I don't have anything left to give."

Declan tucks my head into his chest and rubs my back while I cry. He gives me time to feel my pain, all while sitting right there with me, shouldering the burden if only for a little bit.

Finally, he peels me off his chest and cradles my face in his hands. He looks at me with such intensity, his eyes begging me to listen to his every word.

"I'm not leaving you or Lucas. You're stuck with me, sweetheart. I'm so goddamn sorry your daddy walked out and left you in more ways than one. But I'm not him. I know there's nothing I can say right now that will prove that to you, so I'll just have to keep being here, keep showing up, keep being whatever you need me to be until you trust me. As for the rest? Well, I can't promise I won't die one day. In fact, I'm pretty sure that's inevitable. But you can't let that fear keep you from letting someone in, from letting them love you. If you push me away right now, you're still going to be alone, and I don't want that for you. Or for me. I don't want us to be alone anymore, baby girl. So will you just be here? With me? Let me take care of you, Luna. Let me love you like this," he pleads, wiping away my tears once again.

"Declan," I sniffle.

"Please, baby, just let me take care of you."

His hands slide around my waist, pulling me closer to him, while I loop my arms around his neck. I kiss him with all of my passion, all of my gratitude, all of the words I can't seem to say. I hold on to him like he's the only thing keeping me tethered to earth, and honestly, he just might be.

We finally break apart, gasping for air.

"I'm sorry," I whisper.

"Shh, it's okay, little hummingbird," he says, tucking me back into his chest. "I've got you, sweetheart, I've got you," he whispers while stroking my back.

Chapter 16

Declan

I hold Luna tight in my embrace for a long time, loving the fact that she lets me. Looking down on her now, I know without a doubt that there will never be anyone else for me. I almost told her I love her earlier, and while that's true, she's not ready to hear it yet. Today was already a big day for us.

I knew she'd be upset about me paying off her medical bill, but I had no fucking clue the wrath I would incur in the process. When she insinuated I thought she was a whore, pain like I've never experienced lanced through me. I thought I was going to lose her, so I acted on instinct. I wanted to tie her up and make her listen to me, but I opted to wrap my arms around her and wait out the storm.

She was so fucking broken, so angry and sad and overwhelmed. While I usually love her passion and fight, I don't so much like when it's directed at me. Luckily, she decided to let me in, if only a little bit. When we were in my office today, she told me she trusted me. Her surrender of her body and pleasure pleased me greatly. But tonight, she trusted me with so much more. She opened herself up and trusted me with her complete care, trusted me to provide for her, to be there for her, to love her, even if she doesn't know it yet. I feel more fulfilled right now than I ever have like I finally have a purpose. I swear I won't let her down.

Luna's stomach grumbles loudly, making her giggle. God, I love the sound of her laugh.

"I guess I better feed my little hummingbird, huh?"

"Yes, please," she grins up at me.

I smile and kiss her cute little nose, ridiculously happy that she's showing me this small sign of trust to provide for her basic needs.

After the dinner of chicken alfredo I prepared for us, Luna carries our dishes over to the sink and begins to fill it up with water. I get an image of spending all of our nights like this; me cooking and Luna cleaning, or vice versa, or maybe Luna just sitting on the couch and putting her feet up while I do everything. I wouldn't mind that at all. Suddenly, the picture changes to Luna on the couch reading to our daughter while pregnant with our son.

I never thought I'd want a family of my own, but the thought of Luna pregnant with my kid stirs an unfamiliar longing deep inside of me. I swear I feel tears gathering in my eyes just thinking about it.

"Declan, are you okay?" Luna asks so sweetly from where she's standing at the kitchen sink.

Instead of answering her with words, I get up and slide my arms around her from behind and kiss her neck before resting my head on her shoulder.

"I'm just happy you're here with me. Happier than I have any right to be."

She spins around in my arms and gives me a quick kiss, placing her hands on my chest. Luna laughs and I look down to see bubbles from the dishwater on my shirt. She scoops some up and wipes it on my cheek, giving me a playful smirk.

I reach behind her and gather a handful of soap suds and pile them on her head. She giggles and shakes her head out like a dog, sending the bubbles flying all around us. Before I can stop her, she turns around and scoops up water in her hands and flings it at me. I jump back, though I still get a good amount on my shirt.

I'm momentarily shocked at this turn of events, but I recover quickly.

"Careful, little girl," I growl as I stalk towards her. Luna bites her lip and raises an eyebrow in challenge.

She darts off to the side, trying to get away from me, but I grab a cup she just washed and fill it up with water from the sink and dump it over her head. She shrieks and then belly laughs, wrapping her arms around her tiny waist like she's trying to contain all of her joy.

"I can't believe you did that!" She giggles while wringing out the water from her soaking wet hair.

"I can't believe I didn't think of it sooner. Now I'll have to take you out of your wet clothes until they dry."

Luna tries to get away from me again, but I catch her by her waist and haul her into me for a devastating kiss. She moans as I slip my tongue into her mouth and consume every inch of her. My hands slide down her lithe little body and grip the hem of her baby blue dress, slowly inching it up.

We break the kiss only long enough for me to take her dress off completely and toss it to the side. Luna jumps up into my arms and hooks her ankles together behind my back. I growl and kiss down her neck as she arches her back and presses her body into mine.

"Fuck, I need you," I grunt before nipping at the sensitive skin below her ear.

"I'm yours, sir," she pants, rubbing her hot little pussy over my stomach letting me know she needs me too.

"Take a shower with me." It's not a question, it's a command.

She nods her head and twists her fingers in my hair, pulling me down for another kiss.

I carry her into the bathroom in my bedroom, only breaking the kiss when I set her down on the counter of my double sink. She claws at my shirt and I help her take it off of me. As soon as it's over my head, Luna runs her hands up and down my chest and abs.

"Love your touch, hummingbird. The things you do to me..."

I groan as her hands trail lower and she palms my already hard cock. I step back, chuckling when she scowls at me. Turning on the shower, I adjust the temperature so it's hot, filling up the bathroom with steam.

I quickly get rid of my pants and boxer briefs before returning to undress my little Luna, but I find she's already beat me to the punch.

"Bad girl, you're supposed to let me take off your clothes."

"Oops," she says in a totally fake contrite voice. "Does this mean you'll have to punish me?"

"Fuck," I growl. "Is that what you want? To feel me spank that tight ass of yours?"

She bites her lip and nods, staring me directly in the eyes, challenging me to take her up on her offer.

In one quick move, I spin her around and shove her down on the counter so her ass is presented so beautifully for me. Before she has a chance to protest, I crack my hand over her soft flesh, loving the way it jiggles and turns pink.

Luna cries out in shock and then lets out the sexiest fucking moan.

"Again," she begs.

I wrap her hair around my fist and tug, lifting her head up so she's looking at me in the mirror.

"I'm in control, Luna," I tell her firmly. "Say it."

Her eyes go dark and her nostrils flare. Fucking hell, I love knowing this turns her on as much as it does me. I didn't expect that from someone so inexperienced and young, but it only confirms that she's perfect for me in every way.

"You're in control," she says.

I spank her again, harder this time.

"Who is in control?" Another spank followed by her gasping for air.

"You are, sir, *fuck*, you're in control, sir."

"That's right." I shove two fingers in her soaking wet pussy, never breaking eye contact with her in the mirror.

"Oh!" She cries out at the unexpected invasion. I withdraw my fingers just as quickly and lead her over to the shower, closing the glass door once we're both inside.

Water spills over her hair, shoulders, breasts, and lower. I run my hands up and down her slick body and kiss her roughly.

"You drive me crazy, little hummingbird. Fucking insane," I growl before kissing her again.

My hands find her ass, and I lift her up, pressing her back into the wall. Luna grabs my shoulders and hangs on while I kiss down her neck and rub my cock through the folds of her pussy. I feel her flutter around me, trying to suck me in.

"Your greedy little cunt needs me, doesn't it, Luna?"

"Yes, sir," she moans, throwing her head back and banging it against the wall.

"Careful," I whisper, kissing her cheek.

I continue rubbing my cock through her wet slit, bumping against her clit with each shallow thrust. Luna bucks her hips, trying to position me where she wants me. I sink my teeth into her shoulder, causing her to yelp in surprise.

"I'm in control, little girl," I remind her.

I reposition my hold on her, sliding one hand closer to her center and teasing the split in her cheeks with my fingers. Luna jumps in my arms, making me chuckle darkly. I capture her lips in a scorching kiss while slipping one finger over her tight little rosebud.

"Declan..." she whispers, breaking our kiss.

"Do you trust me?" I ask her, hoping her answer hasn't changed from earlier today.

"Yes, sir. I trust you."

"Good girl."

With that, I thrust my hips and rub my cock on her clit while pressing just the tip of my finger inside of her ring of muscles.

"Oh!" She gasps in surprise. "Oh...my god..." She groans.

"Mmm...you like that, dirty girl?"

"I think I do," she replies in complete surprise.

I wiggle my finger in her ass and slide up just to the first knuckle, and then withdraw. In and out I thrust my finger while stimulating her clit, until I'm in all the way. I position my cock at her entrance, taking my finger out and leaving her empty, loving when she whimpers at the loss.

Then, I slam my dick into her tight pussy while shoving two fingers up her ass.

Luna screams and cums violently in my arms, her pussy and ass clamping down on me.

"Declan, sir, fuck, fuck me, oh fuck," she cries, burying her face in my neck and digging her nails into my shoulder.

"Jesus, woman," I grunt, trying to hold on to my release.

I grind my cock into her cunt, going impossibly deeper. When she's barely recovered from her first orgasm, I pull back and set a relentless pace, fucking her hard. I leave my fingers buried deep in her ass, letting her adjust to the feeling.

"Oh my god, I can't...I'm going to cum again, sir."

"No," I snarl. "Not until I say so."

Luna whimpers and clenches around me, her muscles drawn up tight. I know she's about to explode, but I love seeing her try to keep it at bay.

"Don't you fucking cum, Luna. Don't you dare."

I take my fingers out of her ass and grip both of her cheeks in my hands, tight enough to bruise as I jackhammer in and out of her. Luna lets out these pained moans each time my cock bumps up against her cervix. I feel her pussy flutter, her legs squeezing my hips, her tiny little body shaking with the effort of holding back her orgasm.

"Please, sir, please..."

I withdraw my dick all the way out and then slam into her one last time.

"Cum for me, dirty girl," I growl.

And Jesus, does she cum.

I feel her pussy knot around my cock, squeezing me so damn tight it hurts in the best way. Luna inhales a sharp breath as wave after wave of pleasure wracks her body. She claws at my back, ripping my skin open, making me roar my release and fill her with my seed. I cum so damn hard I feel like I might pass out.

"Breathe," I say to myself as much her.

Luna gasps for air and clings to me as her body trembles with the last of her orgasm. I slide her down my body and hold her close, kissing the top of her head.

When we both have somewhat recovered, I step back and pour body wash into my hands before rubbing it over the dips and curves of her body. Luna leans into me for support, making me smile at how thoroughly fucked and sated she is right now. When I'm done, she soaps me up and places a sweet kiss over my heart.

I cup her face and kiss her deeply, passionately, but slowly. One drugging kiss leads to another and another, and before I know it, I'm spinning her around and placing her hands on the wall.

I sink into her from behind and fuck her slowly with one hand cupping her breasts and the other rubbing circles over her clit. We cum together in a wordless release.

Gathering up her limp body in my arms, I turn off the water and dry us both off before tucking her into my bed and crawling in beside her. I run my fingers through her hair and kiss her forehead until she finally opens her eyes and gives me a shy little smile.

"That was amazing," she whispers.

"Yeah, sweetheart. It was."

She sighs contentedly and I tuck her into my side, running my fingers up and down her back while she traces my tattoos in featherlight touches.

"What does this all mean?" She asks, breaking the silence. "Us sleeping together, you taking care of me, of Lucas too. Are we, like, boyfriend and girlfriend?"

I was thinking about all of this earlier, trying to come up with a way to talk to her about the precarious situation I'm in with the board. Unfortunately, inspiration never struck, so here I am, trying to scramble for words.

"Never mind. I shouldn't have asked," Luna mumbles, trying to roll away from me. I pull her in close, tucking her back into my side where she belongs.

"We're together, baby girl, I already told you that. As for labels, honestly, boyfriend and girlfriend seems so...trivial. But, I'm fine with whatever you want us to be, as long as you're mine and by my side."

This earns me a small smile.

"You're mine, too," she adds.

"Of course. I wouldn't have it any other way." I lean down and kiss the top of her head, steeling myself for this next part. "Our relationship will have...complications, though." Luna stiffens in my arms. "Shit, I'm not saying this right. Remember I told you the board is breathing down my neck about running a tight ship and turning a profit? They want assurance that my brothers and I aren't going to fuck up the company, which includes its public image as well."

"So we have to keep our relationship a secret," Luna says, her voice soft and full of disappointment. Fuck, that tears me up inside.

"I don't want to hide, Luna. I'm not ashamed of you or of us. I just...this company is everything to me and my brothers. It's our legacy."

"I get it."

"Luna..."

"It's okay. I understand. I do." She's trying to put on a brave face, but I know I've hurt her.

"Just for a few months. I promise."

"Okay, Declan."

"Talk to me, hummingbird."

"I'm kind of tired." She yawns and rolls over, facing away from me.

I turn and wrap my arms around her, holding her close.

"Don't leave me, Luna. Give me a chance, just hang in there for a few months and then I promise I'll make it up to you. Please, baby, I need you."

"I need you too," she whispers so quietly I almost don't hear her. I kiss the back of her neck and bury my face in her hair. I can't help but think I just made a huge mistake.

Chapter 17

Luna

Lucas came home the next day and we've been settling into a new routine over the last few weeks. He's currently in a study that includes combining two oral medications to target certain cancer cells. He gets acupuncture twice a week to deal with the aches and pains. During the workday, Lucas is at home doing schoolwork while I'm at the office. Declan plays it cold with me during the day, though he's not nearly as harsh as he was before. But he always makes up for it at night.

We spend most weeknights at my place, cooking dinner and watching TV. Sometimes Declan picks up food or takes Lucas and me out. I spend weekends over at Declan's, though I hardly ever stay the night.

Things are almost perfect; except I can't get what he said out of my mind.

This company is everything to me.

I tried not to let it hurt, but fuck, I felt like my stomach turned to lead. I know I matter to him, and that he truly cares for Lucas and me. But I more than *care* about Declan. I love him. *He's* my everything, and it pains me to know that I'm not the same for him.

I can't compete with his job or with legacy, though I'm trying to understand. He's been working his entire career to build up White Knight Advertising, and now he has the added pressure of living up to his deceased father's expectations, as well as getting approval from the board. It's a lot to take on, so I have to set aside my ridiculous notions of romance.

Declan left two days ago with his oldest brother, Asher, to visit an important potential client in LA. He doesn't usually travel for work but landing this account would be what they need to hit the target to increase profits by twenty percent.

I have been able to work from home these last two days since Declan isn't in the office. He still sends me updates on the potential account and has me organizing notes and listening in on conference calls, but it's been a nice change of pace.

Today, however, I have to go into the office to grab a few other client files and transfer some notes from my laptop to the company server. I shuffle in the office a little after nine. I didn't see the point in scrambling to get here at eight since Declan isn't here and it's barely after six where he's at on the West Coast anyway.

"And where have you been? Wandering off again without notice?" Tiffany greets me as I walk in from the elevator.

"Not that it's any of your concern since you're not my boss, but Declan said I could work from home while he's away on his business trip."

"Of course he did," she scoffs. "You know, you can't keep this up forever."

I spin around and look at her square in the eyes, hoping to convey that I'm not going to let her mess with me.

"No need to be bitter, *Tiff*. You said I wouldn't last long here, but it's over two months later, and here I am, sequined pillows and all."

"Yeah, because you're fucking your boss," she sneers.

I feel the color drain from my face at her words. Tiffany knows she has me on the ropes, try as I might to come up with a convincing protest that doesn't sound whiny or overly defensive.

"I know all about you two," she continues, taking a step towards me and crowding my space.

"I don't know what you think you know—"

"Shut up, you slut," she seethes. "I see the way you look at him like you're in love. But do you know he only looks at you as a man in lust? You're just the flavor of the month."

I don't believe her, of course. Not for a second. Someone as cruel and vindictive as Tiffany could never understand the kind of relationship Declan and I share.

"Nothing is happening between—"

Tiffany whips out her phone and scrolls through, hitting the screen a few seconds later.

"Jesus, Luna. You're so fucking wet. You like being tied up in your boss' office? You like when I spank you and make your pussy drip? Right here in the middle of the workday?"

I break out in a sweat, my heart pounding in my chest as all the air drains from my lungs. It's a recording of that day in Declan's office. We haven't done anything as reckless as that since. In fact, we've hardly been in the same room together since that day.

"How did..."

"I'm not a fucking idiot. When Declan told me to grab him a coffee from a coffee shop twenty minutes away while he had his little *meeting* with you, I set my phone on my desk and hit record. I hoped to maybe get a few screams out of you, but I got so much more. You like it dirty, huh? Do you sleep with all of your bosses? Or, wait, let me guess. You were a *virgin* when you let him fuck you."

My face is burning, tears falling down my cheeks in earnest now.

"Oh my God, you totally were. That's so...perfect," Tiffany laughs cruelly.

I clear my throat and swallow down my absolute terror. I'm glad, not for the first time, that we work up front and that everyone else has offices farther back. Hopefully, no one else can hear this exchange and I can somehow convince Tiffany to keep this between us.

"What do you want?" I ask, trying to sound tough, but failing miserably.

"I want you to quit. If you don't, I'll send this to the board and your precious Declan will lose everything. If you think he'll choose you over his company, you're even more of a fool than I thought."

I try to remain strong, but she hit me right where it hurts. If I cost Declan his company, he'd never forgive me. He already said it was everything to him, and my feelings aside, there's no way I could hurt him like that.

"Okay," I whisper. "I'll quit."

"Today. Right now. Go on, I want to watch you write an email to HR telling them you are quitting."

I do as she says, though every word I type breaks my heart. I have to do this though. For Declan. He's done so much for me already, more than I'll ever be able to repay. I hit send and turn around to see Tiffany tearing down my dry erase board and pictures. She tosses them into a box and then yanks my lava lamp off of my desk, tipping it over and letting the contents spill all over the pink rug I have on the floor.

"Oops!" She says sarcastically.

Tiffany grabs the box for my stuff, walking over to the edge of my desk. In one swift motion, she sweeps her arm across the surface and dumps all of my colorful office supplies into the box, breaking a few more picture frames along the way.

"Here you go," she says way too cheerfully, thrusting the box in my lap.

I have no words, nothing left to say, nothing to do that won't possibly end in damage to Declan and his company. I walk back to the elevator on shaky legs.

***

Lucas is at his acupuncture appointment, which I'm more than grateful for. I need some time to decompress, preferably curled up in my bed with a pint of ice cream and a side of cathartic crying.

By the time I get back to the apartment, I'm completely drained of energy. Looking at my phone, I see I have a text from Declan. Fear spikes my heart, but I realize it's probably just his morning text, seeing how I'm doing. Even though he's been away for a few days, he texts me all the time and we FaceTime every night. The thought of talking to him right now though is unbearably heartbreaking, so I shut off my phone and grab the pint of Ben & Jerry's Cherry Garcia instead. Yeah, it's only ten-thirty a.m., but I think I deserve this.

I must have dozed off, because the next thing I know, I'm startled out of my sleep by something trickling down my chest. Upon further inspection, I see the ice cream has melted and is now pouring down my shirt and onto my bedding. Awesome.

After cleaning up and throwing my sheets in the wash, I look at the clock. It's just about two, which means Lucas should have been home hours ago. What the hell?

I turn on my phone to call Lucas and see I have a few texts and missed calls from Declan, five missed calls from Sarah who took Lucas to his appointment, and two missed calls from the hospital.

"Fuck!" I say into the void.

I call the hospital and try to get my breathing under control. Could this day get any worse? I banish that thought, not wanting to tempt the universe.

I punch in the required numbers in the hospital's automated phone system and am finally directed to the emergency room.

"Come on, come on, pick up already," I grumble impatiently.

"St. Joseph's," the lady on the other end of the line says almost as impatiently as I feel.

"Hi, I'm Luna Foster, my brother Lucas Foster was recently admitted?"

I hear typing and clicking and then she confirms. "Yes, he was brought in several hours ago for severe pain and dehydration. He's in the ICU right now due to his diagnosis. The doctors are running tests."

"Thank you, I'll be right there," I manage to squeak out before hanging up the phone and crumbling apart completely.

"Get it together, you can do this," I tell myself over and over again. I feel overwhelmingly alone, much like the day Lucas first got his diagnosis. I wanted to tell mom about it and have her make it all better. Only this time, I want to tell Declan and have him hold me in his arms.

Not only is he not here, but he might not even want to be with me anymore once he finds out what a liability I am to him and his company. The thought of never seeing him again only adds to my despair, so I have to push that thought aside and once again suck it up so I can be there for Lucas. That's what matters right now.

Twenty minutes later, I storm into the ICU and make my way to his room. Lucas looks pale with sunken eyes. It always shocks me how his health and appearance can change so drastically. Just this morning he was looking almost like his old self, albeit skinnier and a little more fragile.

"Hey," I say quietly when he spots me at the door.

"Luna," he breathes out. "I don't know what happened..."

"Shh, it's alright. Go back to sleep, okay?"

I check his chart and the machines he's hooked up to. He's not doing great, but I try not to let my terror show on my face. Lucas closes his eyes and I slip out to find the doctor on call.

After half an hour of waiting, Dr. Stanhope finally steps in.

"Luna," he nods towards me and then begins studying Lucas' chart.

"Give it to me straight, doc. What's going on?"

"I always did like your tenacity, Luna. I think you're going to need it."

My stomach drops.

"Lucas has a tumor pressing on his lungs, the same one we were keeping an eye on these last few months. It's rare for tumors to be this aggressive with lymphoma, but I think we need to operate on this as soon as possible."

"Yeah, of course, whatever it takes," I tell him, my voice steady as I push the fear and dread aside so my assertive big sister role can take center stage.

"I actually have an opening tomorrow morning at six-thirty."

"Yes, we'll take it."

"You should know there are certain risks involved with surgeries like this..."

I listen while he lists of possible complications, but when he tells me again that his recommendation is for surgery, I don't question it.

Dr. Stanhope leaves shortly after and I prepare for a long afternoon and evening standing vigil by Lucas' bedside. I even turn on the TV and flip to the food network just in case Lucas wakes up.

Chapter 18

Declan

Luna hasn't responded to me in over eight hours. She's not online and she isn't answering my texts or calls. I swear to Christ I'll never forgive myself if something happened to her while I'm on this stupid fucking business trip.

Desperate for some modicum of control over this situation, I call Cooper.

"Declan! Are you enjoying Asher's company?" Cooper asks when he picks up. Normally I'd give him some line and make fun of Asher with him, but I don't have time for that shit, not while Luna could be hurt or in danger.

"Coop. I need you to check on Luna. Is she in the office? Did she come in today?"

"She's your new assistant, right?"

"Yes," I grit my teeth, hoping he doesn't inquire any further.

There's a pause on the other line, and I know he's considering giving me shit. He must hear the seriousness in my tone, however, because he doesn't press the issue.

"Alright. I'll put you on hold and go check on your little assistant. You want me to have her call you if she's there?"

"Take the phone with you. If she's there, put her on."

Again, he pauses, but then I hear him sigh and open his office door. A few moments later, I hear muffled voices, one of which belongs to Tiffany.

"Bro, she quit."

"What?" I roar into the phone.

"Yeah, Tiff said she came in today and just...quit."

What the hell happened? Why won't she talk to me? Something is up and I hate that I'm across the country right now.

"I need you to go to her apartment, Coop," I sigh, knowing this is totally going to blow our cover. I guess it doesn't matter now, since she quit on me. I don't give a shit about any of that though, I just need to know she's okay.

"Dude, are you going to tell me what's going on? I heard she disappeared a few weeks ago and you let it slide. And now this?"

"Weren't you just telling me not all that long ago that I needed to try and have some humanity and understanding?"

"I think we both know this goes beyond that," he counters.

"I fucking love her, Coop."

For the first time, possibly ever, Cooper has no response.

"I didn't mean for it to happen," I continue, hoping to make him understand my desperate need to check up on her. "But she...I don't know. She makes me feel things. Protective. Possessive. Happy."

More silence.

"Holy shit," Cooper finally says. "You love her."

"I know it looks bad, especially with the board—"

"Declan, who gives a fuck about that? You love, which is a miracle in itself, but this person loves your grumpy ass too? Unfuckingbelievable."

"I didn't know you were such a romantic," I quip.

"Ah, but of course. I can't wait to fall in love. I'm tired of playing the field."

"Really?" This comes as a shock to me, but then I snap out of it. Now's not the time for that conversation. "We can talk about it later; I just need you to check on her. I'm worried and I'm stuck here for another day."

"Yeah, of course. I haven't had a chance to properly introduce myself to my future sister-in-law," he chuckles.

I give him her address and hang up, feeling marginally better that Cooper took the news of Luna and me so well.

An hour later, I get a text from Cooper.

Not at her apartment. BTW, you gotta move your girl out of this shit hole.

I'd smile at his natural protective instinct, even over someone who isn't technically family yet, but I'm too fucking pissed and worried and feeling out of control. I hate this. Everything about this.

Call St. Joseph's. Her brother might be there.

A few minutes later, my phone rings.

"They won't give me any information since I'm not family," Cooper says.

"Fuck," I growl, running my free hand through my hair.

"Hey, we'll figure it out."

"I hate this." Silence spreads over us, neither one sure what to do. "I'll be on the next flight," I finally say.

"What are you going to tell Ash?"

"Fuck Asher."

"Hell yeah! That' what I've been saying for *years*."

I manage a chuckle at his response.

"I'll see you soon, Coop. Thanks for this."

"Any time. Seriously. I know these last six months have been hard on all of us, but you know I love you, right?"

"Don't get all mushy on me now," I grunt.

"Alright, fine. I'll save it for when you get back," he teases.

There's a beat of silence over the phone. "I love you too, Coop," I tell him.

"Psh, don't get all mushy on me now."

"Fuck you," I grumble.

Cooper laughs and I hang up on him. Bastard.

***

Twelve fucking hours later, I finally land at JFK. I ditched Ash after our late lunch meeting and haven't answered any of his calls. I sent him a text saying something came up and I had to go back home. I may not particularly like the guy most of the time, but I don't want him to worry.

And he's not worried. He's pissed. That's fine, I'll deal with him later. Right now, I need to find my hummingbird.

I booked the next flight to New York, which meant several long layovers. It's seven a.m. as I step off the final plane and call my driver. I haven't slept all night and I'm feeling it. I know sleep will be impossible until I have Luna in my arms again.

My first stop is Luna's apartment, which is empty. I tell my driver to head to St. Joseph's next. I have a bad feeling, and I will tear down the fucking walls of that hospital to find Lucas and Luna.

I storm through the doors to the main reception area and proceed to argue with the front desk lady who won't give me any information.

"This is fucking bullshit," I grumble to myself while pacing around and calling Luna for the tenth time today. I don't know for certain that she's even here, I just have a hunch that if neither her nor Lucas is at their place, something is wrong.

The front desk lady is eyeing me warily after our latest exchange, but then she turns to help someone else. I take the opportunity to slip into the ICU and wander around as inconspicuously as I can.

No such luck.

Next, I hit up the oncology wing, but don't see any sign of Lucas or Luna. I see a sign pointing towards the surgical wing, and my stomach drops thinking about Lucas going into surgery while Luna waits for him all alone.

I search the waiting room but don't see any sign of Luna. I growl in frustration, earning me a few startled looks from those around me. I'm about to find out who the head of the hospital board is and give a generous donation in exchange for information about Lucas, but then I see Luna come out of the bathroom

My heart beats for the first time since I heard she quit. She doesn't see me at first as I make my way towards her. Luna is always beautiful, but right now she looks so run down, not unlike that night I picked her up and brought her to my home.

When she looks up, fresh tears stream down her face, making me run to close the distance between us. She flings herself into my arms and I scoop her up, squeezing her tightly as she sobs in my arms. I don't know what the fuck is going on, but it doesn't matter as long as I have her here with me.

Reluctantly, I let her go so I can walk us over to a nearby bench on the side of the room, offering us a bit of privacy. Luna moves to sit down next to me, but I grab her hips and guide her so she's sitting in my lap, unwilling to have her that far away from me right now, possibly ever.

"How's Lucas? What happened?"

She sniffles and I wipe away more tears from her beautifully haunted face.

"He has a tumor pushing on his lungs. He came in yesterday and went into surgery a little over two hours ago."

"I'm so sorry I wasn't here, sweetheart. Why didn't you call? Or answer your phone?"

She looks away from me, guilt coloring her features. I reach out and cup her chin, turning her face towards me once again.

"Why did you quit, baby girl?" I ask after she doesn't answer my first set of questions.

Luna sighs and buries her head into the side of my neck. I wrap my arms around her and hold her close.

"Whatever it is, we'll get through it, okay?"

She nods and curls up deeper into my chest. We're silent for a few minutes. I'm not sure what to say to make her talk to me, but if this is what she needs, I can give it to her.

"Tiffany had a recording," she finally says, her voice soft and defeated.

"What?"

"That day in your office when you sent her away for coffee. She left her phone out and recorded us. She said if I didn't quit, she'd release it to the board and you'd lose everything."

"Fuck!" I growl, making Luna tense in my arms. "Sorry, Luna. Fuck, this is my fault. I shouldn't have taken you in my office like that." As soon as the words come out of my mouth, I know they were the wrong things to say. "That came out wrong. What I meant is that I shouldn't have kept us a secret. It was setting us up for something like this, and I'm so sorry you had to deal with this alone. Why didn't you say anything to me? Or tell her to fuck off?"

The more I think about it, the angrier I get. How fucking dare Tiffany threatened my hummingbird? What the hell is her end game? Does she really think I'd choose her just because Luna isn't in the office anymore?

"I would never ruin your career, Declan, especially when you're so close to having everything you've ever wanted."

Her words are so painful I can't even breathe for a second. I lean back and tip her chin up. The look of absolute devotion and yet deep hurt in her eyes fucking guts me.

"Luna, don't you know? *You* are everything I've ever wanted." Another wave of unbearable pain seizes my heart when I see doubt in her eyes.

"But...but that day you told me we needed to keep our relationship a secret, you said the company meant everything to you. You said it was your legacy. I won't destroy that, Declan, you've worked too hard."

"Luna, I was a fucking idiot. Screw the company, my legacy, all of it. I just want you. I need you. I'm so sorry I made you doubt that. You are my heart, little hummingbird."

She cups my face and kisses me, slow and deep. When we break apart, she rests her forehead on mine.

"I didn't know if I'd ever see you again," she whispers.

"You can't get rid of me now, sweetheart. I'm afraid I can't let you go. I won't."

Before she can respond, someone calls out her name. I kiss her forehead and help her up.

"How is he?" She asks.

"He's out of surgery now. Lucas did really well, it's the best we could have possibly hoped for. We removed the tumor and already his vitals are improving."

Luna leans into me, completely devoid of strength. I wrap an arm around her waist and tuck her into my side, holding her up.

"Thank you, Dr. Stanhope," I say.

He nods. "You can see him now if you want. He's still knocked out from the anesthesia, but he should be awake in the next hour or so."

I thank him again and lead Luna towards his room, practically dragging her little body along. She just has to hold on a little longer, then I'll take her home and make her forget about this horrible fucking day. I'll spend the rest of my life making it up to her.

I can't believe how careless I was with my words that night we discussed our relationship. Of course, I didn't mean that the company was everything to me. Has she really thought that the entire time we've been together these last few weeks? I suppose my being cold with her in the office and then warm with her when we were at her place only cemented that thought in her head. God, I am such a fucking fool for ever choosing the company over her.

When we get to Lucas' room Luna slumps against me. I kiss the top of her head and guide her towards the chair next to his bed. Sitting down, I pull her into my lap while she takes a hold of his hand. We sit like that for what feels like an eternity, Luna resting her head on my shoulder and holding Lucas' hand while I stroke her hair and hold her close.

"Luna?" A weak voice floats through the air, causing us both to snap our eyes over to Lucas.

"Hey," she says in a calming voice. "Can I get you some water? The doc says only clear liquids for the rest of the day. I can order some chicken broth and your favorite tea for lunch."

God, she's so strong. I know she's at the absolute end of herself, but she somehow summoned the strength and grace to be everything he needs right now.

"Fuck the food, how are you?" He asks, making me smile. The kid has some fight in him, that's for sure. I love that he's as protective of her as she is of him.

Luna sighs and slips off my lap so she can hug her brother. "Better now that you're awake. Dr. Stanhope says you did really good."

He nods. "You taking care of my sister?" Lucas asks me.

"I'm fine, Lucas," Luna answers for me. "Right now, your health is the most important thing."

"Lulu, I love you," he starts. "But you have to take care of yourself, too." Luna sighs, but Lucas continues. "You," he points to me. "Take her home and make sure she eats something and sleeps."

"Lucas," Luna protests.

"Nuh-uh. No, ma'am. I don't want to see you until tomorrow afternoon. And please, for the love of God, don't go into work tomorrow."

I step in before she can say anything.

"I'll make sure she gets food and sleep, and I'll keep her in bed all day, by any means necessary."

"Oh my god, I do *not* want to hear that," Lucas whines, but I see a smile tugging on his lips.

Luna, on the other hand, looks absolutely mortified. Lucas and I share a look, and I know it's time to go.

Chapter 19

Declan

Once we get back to my penthouse, I scoop Luna up and place her on the counter in my bathroom while I run a bath for us. I gently strip her of her clothing and place her in the tub. She doesn't say anything, she just brings her knees up to her chest and wraps her arms around her legs.

She looks so small and so vulnerable right now. All I want in the whole world is to hold her and shield her from every bad thing.

So, I do.

I rid myself of my clothes and get in the tub behind her, coaxing her to lean back against me. She does so without protest, and I wrap my arms around her, nuzzling into the top of her head and breathing her in. Even after the long night in the hospital, she still smells like my Luna. Citrus and vanilla and mine.

"I'm so sorry, hummingbird. So fucking sorry."

"It's okay, you're here now."

"It's not okay. Did you spend the last few weeks thinking the company was more important to me than you?"

She shrugs in my arms and I squeeze her tighter.

"That's the furthest thing from the truth, Luna. I was thoughtless with my words and I'm so sorry I hurt you. If it ever came down to it, I would choose you over the company every time, hummingbird."

She turns in my arms and kisses me. It's slow and sweet and full of promises.

I gently turn her back around and begin washing her body, taking inventory of every curve, every inch of her smooth skin. All of it is mine. Mine to protect, mine to love, mine to cherish.

When I'm done, I dry us off and carry Luna to bed, snuggling in behind her and holding her close. "Get some sleep, my little hummingbird," I murmur before placing soft kisses on the back of her neck and shoulder.

"Mmhmm," she mumbles, already halfway there. I smile and bury my face in her hair, breathing in her scent and letting it consume me while I hold her in my arms.

I stay with her for a while, just watching over her as she sleeps. Finally, I roll over and look at the clock. Two p.m. Just enough time to put my plan into action.

I slip out of the room and call Cooper.

"Declan, did you find your girl?" He asks as soon as he picks up the phone.

"Yeah, she was at the hospital with her brother."

"Oh shit, everything okay?"

"Yeah, it will be. She's resting at my place now."

"Good, good. So, what's up? Did you find out why she quit?"

"Yes," I growl. "That's why I'm calling. First of all, Tiffany needs to be fired. Immediately."

"Okaaaay...I mean, no big loss there. I certainly won't miss the way she throws herself at all of us even though I'm pretty sure no one has taken the bait. Wait, do you think Ash slept with her at some point?"

"No way, you know his policy on office romance. And women in general."

"No relationships, no attachments. Pretty sure that's how he feels about everybody though."

I sigh and think about Ash. If I was a cold bastard before Luna came into my life, Ash is like the Arctic tundra.

"We can worry about him later, right now I need your help. Especially in convincing Ash about what I need to do next."

"You know I love any opportunity to go toe to toe with Asher."

"I don't want a big, blow-up fight. I need us to be a united front on this."

"Uuuuugggggghhhh," Cooper sighs exasperatedly. "Maybe just a little yelling? And a sprinkle of snark?"

I chuckle over the phone. I really have missed the kind of easy relationship Cooper and I had back in the day. But right now I need to convey the importance of all of us getting on the same page.

"Look, this is serious, Coop. Tiffany has a recording of Luna and me. In my office."

"Oh ho ho, no way! I knew you were filthy. Good job, brother, that's fucking hot."

I growl into the phone.

"Dude, chill. I just didn't think you had it in you."

"Anyway," I continue, a little more annoyed than before. "She threatened Luna with it and made her quit. The thing is, I doubt that will be enough for her. I have a feeling she's going to the board anyway. We need to get ahead of this thing, you know?"

"Shit, Declan, that's fucked up. Is Luna okay?"

"What do you think? She's shaken up and it made her doubt my feelings for her."

Cooper laughs over the phone. "I'm still not used to you having any feelings at all."

"Yeah, well..." I don't really know how to respond to that.

"Hey, it's a good thing. I always felt left out of the soulless billionaire brother's club with you and Asher. It's nice having you on my side."

"There are no sides, Cooper. Or, at least I hope there aren't anymore. I'm sorry you felt like the odd man out."

Cooper is silent for a moment. "Holy shit, dude. Are you apologizing?"

"Yeah, yeah, fuck off," I grumble.

"Hey, it's great. Luna worked some magic on you. God knows I tried to get you to loosen up and give a shit about something other than pleasing dad and building the company. I'm just happy for you. For real."

He sounds sincere, almost wistful. I remember something he said over the phone yesterday. *I can't wait to fall in love. I'm tired of playing the field.*

"Are you seeing anyone?" I ask, realizing I don't know much about my brother anymore, but hoping to find out more.

"Nah, I'm kind of tired of the women throwing themselves at me just cuz all of us make the most eligible whatever-the-fuck list every year. It was fun at first, but now it's just...I don't know. I just want to mean something to someone, you know?"

"Damn, Coop. That's heavy." He's always been more in touch with his feelings, sure, but he's usually the comic relief, the goofball.

"Yeah, well, it's whatever. I'm just looking for something real."

"Sure, yeah. I get it. I mean, I didn't know that's what I was looking for until I met Luna, but now... Well, now I can't picture my life without her."

"Aww, Declan! My little baby is all grown up and ready to settle down and shit!" He laughs. "Are you going to lock it down? Get a ring and promise forever?"

"That's part of the plan, yeah. But I need your help."

We spend the next hour calling the necessary people and setting up the pieces. Hopefully, by tonight I can offer the kind of life my little Luna deserves, without any obstacles in the way.

Chapter 20

Luna

I wake up warm and cozy, with the now-familiar peppermint and pine scent of Declan all around me. I'm in his bed, which means I didn't just dream him storming into the hospital yesterday and holding me. And he really did tell me I'm more important than his company, that I'm *everything*

I roll over to snuggle up with him, but frown when he's not there. I do, however, see a note on the nightstand, next to the clock, which reads six-thirty p.m. Jeez, I guess I really did need to sleep.

Sitting up, I reach for the note and smile as I read over the words.

My beautiful hummingbird,

I had to step out and take care of a few things. There is a snack in the kitchen for you. I won't be back till later this evening, but I know I'm thinking about you always.

Yours,

Declan

I remember the other note he left me, that first morning I woke up in his guest room. He signed off in the same way. *Yours.* I didn't believe it then, but I do now. He's mine in every way, and I'm his.

I wander out into the kitchen and see a tray of scones - chocolate chip, of course. He knows me well. If there's an option between fruit and chocolate, I'll choose chocolate every time.

After eating two scones, I decide to start a fire and find a good book to read to take my mind off of whatever Declan is out doing.

Before long, the elevator doors ding, signaling Declan will be walking in any second.

"God, it's good to come home to you, hummingbird," he says, leaning against the doorway of the living room.

I can't help but smile. He seems exhausted, but not anxious or upset with me. I, however, still have questions. "What are you going to tell the board?" I blurt out. "I mean, sorry, I...what does all of this mean? Are we still a thing? Do you want to keep us a secret?"

"Luna..." He tries to say something, but I can't seem to stop the word vomit.

"Does that bitch Tiffany still work there? You know she won't stop. She's going to ruin everything for you!"

"Luna, let me explain everything, okay?"

I nod wring my hands in my lap as he makes his way over to me. When he sits down, he takes my hands in his, calming me with just that touch.

"I talked to the board already. That's what I was doing this afternoon. Cooper supported me, and we even got Asher to agree to a united front."

"United front about what?"

He leans forward and kisses me on the forehead, breathing me in. He pulls away but cups my chin in one hand so I have to look at him.

"I told the board that I fell in love with my gorgeous, captivating, strong, intelligent assistant and that she's going to be my wife and the mother of my children, and if they have a problem with that, I will step down."

My head spins with his confession. I still have questions, but there's only one I need the answer to.

"You love me?" I whisper, still in disbelief of how everything is unfolding.

"I love you so much, Luna. I love you in a crazy, undeniable, overwhelming way that I can't explain, but it's so fucking real."

Tears form and fall from my eyes as I nod. "So real," I agree before welcoming his sweet kiss on my lips. Declan tucks some of my hair behind my ear and then cups the back of my neck, pulling me deeper into his kiss as his tongue seeks entrance.

I open up for him and moan softly as his tongue drags along the sensitive roof of my mouth. I feel more than hear a deep chuckle bubble up from his chest. Then, Declan leans into me and lays me down on the couch, pinning my wrists above my head with one hand while continuing to kiss his way down my neck.

He leans back and looks at me, smiling softly with such adoration in his eyes. My heart goes to complete mush for this man who somehow found me worthy of letting into his life. Declan bends his head down and kisses my hairline. I feel a cool band slip over the ring finger of my left hand and gasp.

Declan lets my wrists go, and I bring my hand down to look at the gorgeous ring he just put on my finger. It's a pear-cut diamond in a rose gold setting with smaller diamond clusters on either side. It's beautiful and not gaudy or over the top. It's perfect.

I glance back up at Declan, who is holding himself above me and looking at me with such love swimming in those gray eyes of his.

"Well, not that you asked me, but yes, I'll marry you," I manage to say before the happy tears come in full force and choke me up.

He grins and kisses my lips and then trails kisses down my jaw and nips my pulse point.

"Damn right you'll marry me, hummingbird. I wasn't going to accept any other answer," he whispers.

The next thing I know, Declan flings me over his shoulder, making me squeal.

"Hey! That's no way to treat your future wife!" I shout, pounding on his back as he makes his way towards the bedroom.

Declan swats my ass, making me squeal again. "Oh, I know *exactly* how I want to treat my future wife tonight," he growls. God, I love when he takes charge like this. My pussy grows wet as I imagine all the dirty things Declan has in store.

He sets me down on the floor in front of the bed and kisses me hard and fast before pulling away.

"Strip for me, baby girl, and then crawl on the bed. I want you naked and on your back."

A tingle of pleasure ripples over my skin and sinks deeper into my core at his command.

"Yes, sir," I say, my voice low and full of need.

Declan growls and watches me take off my clothes for a moment before he turns around to grab something from the drawer of his dresser. I climb on the bed like he told me to and stretch out on my back, completely naked. A shiver runs through me as I wait for Declan to join me.

I feel the bed dip down with his weight. Declan straddles me, though he's still fully clothed. He leans down and kisses me while lifting both of my hands over my head. When he breaks the kiss, I feel something soft and silky wrap around my wrist. I gasp and look up, my heart pounding in my chest as I watch him tie my wrist to the headboard.

Declan trails his finger down the inside of my arm and strokes my cheek. "Do you trust me, little Luna?"

"Yes," I breathe out.

Declan pinches my nipple, making me whimper.

"Yes, who?"

"Yes, sir."

"Good girl. My good, dirty girl."

He ties my other wrist, and then moves to tie my ankles to the bed as well. I test my new restraints, noting that they aren't too tight. My heart is pounding, a little from nerves, but mostly from excitement. I'm spread out and tied down for Declan, *my* Declan, to do whatever he wants to me.

Declan straddles me again and smiles, though it's not his sweet smile of adoration from earlier. No, this smile is dark, full of hunger and deep need. He slips a silk blindfold over my eyes, throwing my world into complete blackness.

I feel him lean down and brush his lips against mine before he leaves the bed entirely. The only thing I can hear is the sound of my heart rattling in my chest and my shallow breaths. My body trembles for his touch, the anticipation killing me.

His finger brushes against my collarbone, making me jerk in response. "So beautiful, spread out for me like this. I'm going to devour you, little Luna. Every inch of you."

Declan trails his finger down the center of my chest, drawing a line from the valley of my breasts down to my belly button. Then it's gone.

Suddenly, I feel his warm breath on my breast as he licks my nipple once and then pulls away. His lips ghost down the curve of my waist and stop at my hip so he can nip the tender skin there.

I never know where his next touch is going to be, but he teases me with his teeth and tongue and fingers, grazing over my neck, torso, thighs, calves, and everywhere in between. He truly is devouring me. Everywhere he makes contact burns for more.

I try to clench my thighs together to ease some of the throbbing pressure in my pussy, but my legs are spread too far apart. Declan notices my efforts and chuckles before latching on to my breast with his mouth.

I gasp and bow my back off of the bed. His hand reaches up to cup my other breast and pinch the nipple.

"Oh, god," I moan. Everything is heightened, every touch going straight to my clit.

I feel his other hand skim up the insides of my thighs. He groans into my chest as his fingers scoop up the juices trailing down my thighs.

"You like this, dirty girl? Your cunt is dripping, crying out for me."

"Yes, fuck yes, sir, I need you."

Declan switches breasts, sucking on the other one now while his fingers continue inching up my thigh. I feel them brush against my slit and cry out. Just as quickly, they move away.

"Nooo!" I whine.

Declan chuckles darkly. "Greedy little Luna. What am I going to do with you?"

"Fuck me, sir, please fuck me," I beg, wiggling my hips and pulling against my restraints.

"Hmm... I could," he says while dipping two fingers into my pussy, gathering up my honey. I gasp and pull against the ties around my wrists and ankles. "I could stuff you full of my fat cock, drive into this sweet, tight pussy of yours again and again." He thrusts his fingers into my entrance all at once, hard and fast, again, fucking me with his hand while his thumb swirls around my clit.

Fuck, I'm already so worked up from all of his teasing I think I'm going cum already.

Then, as quickly as it began, he pulls his fingers out of me, leaving my pussy empty and sucking around nothing. I grunt in frustration and then cry out when Declan pinches my nipple. Hard. It hurts in the best way, releasing a flood of sensations that has me gushing.

"You take what I give you, Luna. Do you understand?"

I whimper and nod, but Declan pinches and twists my nipple again. "Tell me. Tell me you understand," he growls.

"Yes! Yes, sir, I understand."

He kisses me then, sucking my tongue into his mouth and dominating me, body and soul. His fingers go back to my pussy and he plays with me, teases me, rubs me up and down, circling my clit and working me up, only to move his hand away before I can cum.

"Please! I need to cum." I can't help it; I *ache* for my release.

Declan smacks my clit and I cum instantly, a flood of wetness pouring out of my pussy. I pull against my restraints, my muscles tensing and convulsing, stretching almost painfully and making everything more intense.

"Again," he grunts before smacking my clit again.

I scream and convulse as a second orgasm devastates me. Declan rubs my clit, making me jump and twitch as I try to move away from his hand.

"Too much," I whimper.

"You wanted to cum, so cum for me, Luna."

He pinches my swollen clit, and I feel like I'm peeing. Embarrassment courses through me, but I can't stop, I just keep twisting and more wetness flows out of me as I gasp for air.

"Fucking hell, you're squirting all over me, you filthy, sexy girl. I was going to wait but I can't..."

He growls and then I feel his mouth on my pussy, sucking down everything I'm giving him, grunting and humming into my cunt as he laps and licks me clean.

My thighs quake, trying to close and push him out, but he keeps going. Sweat coats my body and I feel like I'm fighting for every breath. Declan swipes his tongue from my little rosebud all the way to my clit, gathering the last of my juices. He places one last kiss over my mound, and then I don't feel him anymore.

I do, however, hear his zipper and belt, and I can only imagine him stripping down, that gorgeous, sculpted body of his rippling with muscle, and his huge cock standing proudly. Fuck, I just came three times, but picturing Declan naked has me ready for more of whatever he has to give.

Declan kisses my right ankle and unties me before moving on to the other one. Slowly, he kisses a trail up the inside of my leg, ghosting his lips across my over-sensitized skin. My body shakes when he gets to my core, my pussy twitching, and flooding as his warm breath teases my swollen folds. Declan licks up my slit and sucks my clit into his mouth, making me whimper.

Then he releases me, continuing on his tortuous path up my body. I feel him nip the underside of my right breast, and then my left before licking between them, up, up, up, and biting my neck.

"Oh!" I cry out in surprise. Declan chuckles darkly and then thrusts his tongue inside of my mouth at the same time his huge cock slams into me, hitting home in one hard thrust.

"Jesus, Luna..." he growls.

He sets a relentless pace and I wrap my legs around his hips, bucking and writhing underneath him, urging him deeper. One hand trails down the side of my body and then he grips my ass, squeezing hard. He stills my movements, holding me in place and fucking me so damn rough.

I didn't think I could cum again, and certainly not so soon, but I feel the pressure building up in my lower belly. Declan kisses me hungrily, biting my bottom lip and grunting into my mouth each time he thrusts inside of me. He kisses down my jaw and nips my earlobe.

"You make me crazy, little Luna. Fucking insane. I want to possess you, destroy you, rebuild you. I want to fuck you and tear your little pussy to shreds until you cum so hard the only thing you'll remember is my name. Do you know why? Because you're mine, every fucking inch. Now cum for me, my dirty fucking girl."

He twists his hips and thrusts into me, hitting my g-spot at the same time his teeth sink into my neck.

I gasp and moan at how primal it is, his need to mark me. I feel his muscles flexing on top of me as he grinds his cock over my most sensitive spot. And then I cum, god do I cum, so hard it rips through me and leaves my back arched, my body strung tight, my hips aching from being spread so wide. Pleasure floods out from my very core and drips out of me, tickling my ass as my cum trickles down. My orgasm passes through me so violently my head spins and I pass out for a second. And then I remember to breathe.

When I come to, Declan has untied my wrists and taken off the blindfold. He's nuzzling my neck, kissing over the marks he left on me.

"Beautiful, so goddamn beautiful," he mumbles into my skin.

Before I have a chance to fully recover, Declan flips me over onto my belly and pulls my hips up and back. I push myself up on shaky arms and look over my shoulder at him. Declan's eyes are almost black, and his cock is hard and angry looking, slick from me coming all over him.

"Ready, baby?"

I don't think I can take any more, my pussy is beaten up and swollen, yet still dripping and clenching, feeling empty without him. I bite my lip and nod.

Declan smacks my ass, and that does it. I'm ready for more, so much more.

"Tell me. Tell me how much you want it, little Luna."

"God, I want you so bad, I ache, I'm so empty, please, sir, fuck me, fill me, please!" I moan, meaning every single word.

"Fucking Christ," he grunts. Declan's hips snap against my ass and I feel his thick dick enter me once again.

He grips my hips, digging his fingers in and bouncing me off of his cock. I whimper each time he fills me, stretches me, and claims me over and over. I climb higher and higher, his dick driving deeper and deeper, and just as I'm about to explode for the fifth fucking time, Declan pulls out.

"Noooo!" I half whine, half moan in frustration.

Declan leans over me, his sweaty front covering my slick back. He kisses the back of my neck and brushes his lips up against my ear as one hand slides between us to tease my back entrance.

I gasp as the tip of his finger slides inside, the tight ring of muscles clamping down on him.

"Every inch, Luna. Every fucking inch of you is mine," He whispers.

Declan sits up and drags his fingers through my dripping pussy, scooping up my juices and dragging them back to my tight asshole. I feel the swollen head of his cock nudge at my back hole and I hold my breath, shaking with tension and anticipation.

Declan grips my ass cheeks and pulls them apart, pressing his cock farther into me, though he hasn't entered me yet.

"Relax, baby. Breathe for me. I promise you'll like this. You'll beg for it. Trust me, Luna. Trust that I'll always take care of you."

I let out the breath I was holding and focus on relaxing my muscles. There's an intense pressure, and then the tip of his cock pops into my ass, stretching me as he surges forward.

"Luna, fuck, you're so tight..." he groans, inching forward ever so slowly.

It burns and tingles, but also sends jolts of electricity through my body as his cock slides across nerves I didn't know I had. I moan and clamp down when he pulls out of me, and then scream when he slams all the way in.

"Oh my god! Declan!"

"Jesus, I can't...goddamn, you feel so good.

"Fuck me, please fuck me, sir."

Declan roars as he pistons in and out of my ass, one hand sliding around my hips and blurring over my clit. I throw my head back and cry out then he thrusts three fingers into my pussy, fucking me with his hand and his cock. It's too much, too fucking much, my body spasming and clenching up tight.

We're both grunting as we rock into each other. I meet him thrust for thrust, completely lost in absolute bliss. My orgasm slams into me unexpectedly, shaking me to my very core. My arms and legs give out as I sob and convulse. I'm flat on the bed, and Declan lays on top of me, still buried deep in my ass.

"God, Luna, holy shit, you're amazing," he grits out as he grinds down on me.

I feel his cock twitch, which sends a tremor throughout my body. I bury my face in a pillow and fist the sheets in my hands, feeling like I'm going to get lost in absolute rapture.

"Goddamn, baby girl." It sounds like a blessing as he grunts his release. I feel his cum spreading into me like warm honey. He slams into me one last time as I gasp and then break into wordless pleas of pain and pleasure. I have no language left, only sounds.

Declan collapses on top of me and rolls us to the side. I immediately curl up into a ball, feeling wrung out and intensely vulnerable for some reason. I'm still shaking when Declan wraps his arms around me and curls his body around mine.

He kisses a line from the back of my neck to the space in between my shoulder blades. Those soft touches bring me back from the edge, back into his arms, grounding me and reminding me I'm safe with him.

"Are you alright, hummingbird? God, I fucked you so hard, I was so rough with you. I'm sorry, baby."

He turns me so I'm facing him and presses his lips into my forehead.

"I'm okay, Declan. It was intense. But so good. I wanted it. I want you, always," I tell him honestly. "I know I'm safe with you," I add.

He tucks my hair behind my ear and slides his hand to the back of my neck, tilting my face up to meet his gaze. Declan searches my eyes for the truth and then kisses me so sweetly before resting his forehead on mine.

"You're incredible, Luna," he whispers.

I reach out and cup his face in my left hand, and then smile when I see the light reflect off of my ring. He takes my hand in his and kisses the ring before putting my hand back on his face.

"I love you, Declan. I kinda forgot to say that part before," I giggle.

"Mmm, you better love me, little Luna. Cuz I'm so far gone for you. Love you so fucking much, with everything in me. You're my whole world, baby girl, and I'm keeping you forever."

"Forever," I agree.

We stay wrapped up in each other's arms for a while, drifting in and out of sleep. Finally, I nudge Declan awake. He smiles sleepily with his eyes still closed, and I swear my heart skips a beat. He's mine, all mine, and I can't wait for the rest of our lives.

"What's up?" He asks.

"Um, well, you never really told me what happened with the board. I got kind of distracted."

This makes him open his eyes and smirk at me before kissing me deeply. "For the record, I plan on distracting you a lot, little hummingbird."

He leans in for another kiss, but I swat him away. Declan pouts, which might be the most adorable thing in the world, but I hold strong. He sighs and sits up a bit, leaning on the headboard. I sit up with him, and he tucks me into his side.

"Well," he starts. "Not that I give a fuck what the board thinks, but they said they like the image of the new CEO being a family man, settling down and all of that. I still have a position in the company, and you do too if you want it. But you can do anything you want, Luna. Go back to school, get another job, stay home and have ten children..."

"Ten?!"

He chuckles and kisses my temple. "We can start with one."

"I think I can manage that," I say right before yawning.

Declan kisses the tip of my nose and wraps me up in his arms as we sink back into the bed.

"Thanks for taking care of me," I whisper as I snuggle deeper into his embrace.

"Always, my little hummingbird. Always."

Epilogue

I twirl my brand-new wife in my arms and get lost in her brilliant smile. I swear she's glowing. If you told me eight months ago I'd be dancing with my assistant at our wedding in a room full of pink glitter, I'd have laughed and told you to get the fuck out of my face.

But now...well, now I can't imagine my life any other way. Luna and Lucas moved in with me the day after I proposed. I handed Luna my credit card and told her to redecorate the place.

I assumed she'd go with rainbow colors and sequins, but she stuck with more neutral colors. Well, neutral for Luna. Yellow and gray, with a few accents in teal. And there are some sequin pillows, but she confined them to our room. Not that I would care one way or the other if she had the walls painted with pink glitter as long as I have her with me, in my space, all the time.

I've always been protective and a little obsessive with Luna, but I thought after we said our vows and signed our license, I might ease up a bit. The opposite is happening, however.

Holding Luna close, I have the overwhelming urge to tuck her into my side and usher her out of here so I can lock her up in our room and worship her sexy little body. I also want to hold her and rub her back and wrap her up in a soft blanket. Every possessive instinct inside of me is going into overdrive, and I can't seem to help it.

"Hey, are you okay?" Luna asks, her sweet voice filtering in and breaking up my thoughts.

"Yeah. Yeah. I just...I feel insane right now with this need to keep you safe."

"You already do that," she smiles up at me so sweetly.

"I know, I can't explain it. Something lately has just made me crazy possessive."

Luna grins and looks like she's about to burst with happiness. "Could it maybe be because you're going to be a daddy in about eight months?"

Her words slam into my chest and squeeze my heart until it stops completely. And then it beats in overtime, knowing its only job now is to provide for and protect my family.

I drop to my knees in front of her and kiss her belly over her beautiful, sparkling dress. I'm still at a loss for words as a sense of deep joy overtakes me. Luna reaches down and cups my face, wiping away tears I didn't know were there.

Standing, I sweep her up into my arms and kiss her soundly, hoping to convey all of my scattered emotions. When I pull back, she's got that radiant smile on her lips, her eyes shining with tears of her own.

"Are you happy?" She asks.

I swallow around the lump in my throat. "Happier than I ever thought I'd be, hummingbird. God, I love you so much. You and our little one."

"We love you too," she whispers before kissing me again.

"Do you think anyone would notice if we snuck out right now?" I ask, only half-joking. "I want to make love to the mother of my child, my wife, my love."

Luna blushes and bites that damn lip of hers, which doesn't help my cock already lengthening and hardening in my pants. I hold her close, letting her feel my need.

"Declan!" She whisper-yells, making me chuckle. "We haven't even cut the cake yet!"

"People can cut their own cake," I mumble while nuzzling the side of her neck. God, her citrus scent is overwhelming me, and I want nothing more than to lick it off of her.

She swats me away, making me growl softly. Luna puts her hands on her hips and looks adorably indignant.

"This cake is one-of-a-kind, from that little bakery I told you about. Plus, you know how serious I am about my sugar intake. And now that I'm eating for two..."

I can't help but kiss her again. She melts against me but then pulls away.

"Fine, one piece of cake and then you're mine," I compromise.

"I'm already yours, sir," she purrs.

"Fuck, you're not helping, you little minx."

Luna just laughs and drags me along towards the cake table while I try to discretely adjust myself.

I catch sight of Cooper standing by the cake table and staring off towards the back door, a stupid happy grin on his face.

"What's going on with you?" I ask once we reach the table.

"I just met my future wife," he says, still in a daze.

"Really?!" Luna says excitedly. "How romantic! Who is she?"

"I have no fucking clue, but I'll find out by the end of the week."

I clap him on the shoulder and grin. I never believed in love at first sight, but that was before I met my little Luna. I think I knew that first time she stepped into my office that I loved her, but it took me too damn long to figure it out. I'm happy that Cooper doesn't seem to have the same reservations I did.

"Lulu!" Lucas calls out as he heads our way. "It's about damn time you got to the cake. I'm starving!"

"Uh-huh," she rolls her eyes. "Was the steak dinner not enough for you?"

He shrugs. "What can I say? I'm a growing boy. And I have a big paper due on Monday, so I need the extra energy." Lucas grins, and Luna tries for all of two seconds to hide her smile. She's so proud of him, and I am too.

Lucas finished the last round of his treatment a few months ago, and he's been cancer-free ever since. He was able to finish up his high school credits early thanks to doing them online, and both he and Luna enrolled in college classes last month. We offered for Lucas to stay with us, but he wanted to have the full college experience and live in the dorms.

I lean down and kiss Luna's neck. "The faster we cut the cake, the faster I can get you out of here and bury myself in that sweet little pussy of yours," I whisper into her ear.

She blushes bright red and then grins at me.

"I do *not* want to know what you just said, but I think it's time you kids cut the cake and get out of here," Lucas says.

"Couldn't agree more," I tell him.

Luna rolls her eyes, but smiles at me, her eyes soft and bright. God, she's beautiful.

We cut the cake and I feed Luna her first bite, careful not to mess up her makeup or ruin her dress. Luna, on the other hand, smashes cake all over my face and giggles. I lean in and rub my frosting-covered nose all over her face, making her giggle even more.

"You're going to pay for that, baby girl," I growl into her neck where I'm trailing more frosting over her skin. "I'm thinking a nice hard spanking might be the first thing we do when we get to our room."

"I was thinking maybe we could bring some cake up to the room and find some creative ways to use the frosting…"

"Fuck, you're asking for it, dirty girl. You want me to tie your hands behind your back while you lick frosting off of my—"

"Declan!" She whispers, her eyes wide in disbelief. I just grin at her and lick the frosting off of her neck.

"Time's up, sweetheart. Gotta get you naked and in bed as soon as fucking possible."

"You're so bossy," she replies, smiling at me the whole time.

"I think you like it," I counter.

"Maybe we need to test that theory a few more times…"

I kiss her then, tasting her sugary lips and sweet submission. She's so damn perfect, and all mine. Forever.

Also by Cameron Hart

Check out my other popular series and books!
Mafia, MC, & Bodyguard Romance:
<u>Moscatelli Crime Family Series</u>[1]
<u>Di Salvo Crime Family Series</u>[2]
<u>Chaos MC series</u>[3]
<u>Savage Ride</u>[4]
Mountain Man Romance:
<u>Men of Blackthorne Mountain Series</u>[5]
<u>Bear's Tooth Mountain Men Series</u>[6]
Cowboy & Small Town Romance:
<u>Roped in by Love Series</u>[7]

---

1. https://books2read.com/u/mqBaze

2. https://books2read.com/u/m0odzW

3. https://books2read.com/u/bMVAOk

4. https://books2read.com/u/bMVlG7

5. https://books2read.com/u/3RYDvB

6. https://books2read.com/u/mVel7A

7. https://books2read.com/u/3RYlBY

About the Author

Hello. I'm Cameron Hart, and I write sweet steamy romances. I'm a *USA Today* Bestselling author with over forty books available. I write romance with lots of heat, plenty of sweet, and just enough drama to keep things interesting. I graduated from the Iowa Writer's Workshop in 2012 with a degree in creative writing. When I'm not working on my next book, I can be found reading, crocheting, doing yoga, and chasing around my grumpy cats.

What to expect from a Cameron Hart book: Lots of heat, plenty of sweet, and just enough drama to keep things interesting. No cheating, safe, guaranteed HEA!

Read more at https://cameronhart.net/.

www.ingramcontent.com/pod-product-compliance
Lightning Source LLC
Chambersburg PA
CBHW061452150726
47987CB00001B/413